Reviews

GW00871019

Rich Maltzman, PMP, Co-Author of Green Project Management, PMI Cleland Award for Literature, 2011

'I really enjoy this book, both as a parent and Project Manager. Watching my daughter immerse herself in the story and seeing her really appreciate the value of working together and appreciating everyone's strengths was something very special for me. Well done!'

Tony Adams, MPM – (43)

'I love this book and was hooked from the first chapter! Cool characters and a storyline that really draws you in! I also like understanding what my dad does more. Thanks Gary and I can't wait for the next story!'

Talia Adams – (age 10)

The Ultimate Tree House *Project*

Gary M. Nelson, PMP

Illustrated by Mathew Frauenstein

Print ISBN-10: 1482558130
Print ISBN-13: 978-1482558135

This is a work of fiction. Names, characters, businesses, places, events and incidents are either the products of the author's imagination or used in a fictitious manner. Any resemblance to actual persons, living or dead, or actual events is purely coincidental.

This book is designed to provide helpful information to our readers. All processes and procedures described in this book are of a conceptual nature and are not prescriptive; if you would like to build a tree house yourself, there are how-to resources and templates available online that you can refer to (over 63 million references for "tree house" on Google and counting!)

Safety first! Always use appropriate protective gear when handling tools and materials. Talk to a parent or qualified person for help if you ever need First Aid advice or assistance for any reason.

Neither the publisher nor the author shall be liable for any physical, psychological, emotional, financial, or commercial damages, including, but not limited to, special, incidental, consequential or other damages. Our views and rights are the same: You are responsible for your own choices, actions, and results.

Dedication

For my two youngest children, Liam & Daniel, for helping me choose the project for the book and testing the story for me. Comments like "You can't start on the adventure in the first chapter, Dad - you need to introduce the characters more first!" helped to make this a much better book than I started with.

For my wife Lorna, for encouraging me to finally write a children's book.

The Ultimate Tree House *Project!*

Acknowledgements

To my illustrator, Mathew Frauenstein, who is quite a talented artist (and 15 years old when this book was written) - thank you and well done!

To Robin Mills, Natalie Jones and Alex Griffiths of Puketaha Primary School – thank you for your help as I was getting started on the book – your advice is reflected in these pages.

I would also like to thank my proof-readers, Kathleen Hall and Chris Pemberton.

Special thanks to the kids of St Andrews Cub Pack for listening to the story as it grew – some of you went on to start your own tree houses over the summer, and some of you *do know how* to make rope ladders!

Gary Nelson, PMP

Hamilton, New Zealand

March, 2013

The Ultimate Tree House *Project!*

Contents

The Ultimate Tree House *Project!*

1. Spring Break is Over!

"Have a good day at school, James!" called out his mother as he closed the front door.

What was so good about it? James thought. *Spring Break is over, it's back to school and homework.* He sighed and crossed the quiet street in front of his house, kicking a small bit of gravel as he went.

He slowly trudged through the park on his way over to school. He always cut through the bit by the playground because it was shorter. Today, though, he was not in a hurry. *Spring Break is never long enough!* James thought.

The weather was just starting to get nice, and the last of the snow had melted away weeks ago. A few small flowers were starting to poke up through the grass. *Crocuses*, his mother called them. He tested the seat of the swings,

3

to have one more bit of fun before he had to go to class. The seats were still wet from last night's rain. He shrugged and continued walking. With a sigh, he left the park and crossed the road to his school, J. P. Watson Primary School.

His new shoes crunched loudly in the gravel of the schoolyard. He had grown again, his Mom said, and his old shoes were getting too tight. He didn't like new shoes - they were too shiny, and the other kids picked on you if you had new shoes. They usually stepped on your feet. He absently dug his shoes into the gravel to try to rough them up a bit, so hopefully nobody would notice.

He stopped to look at his reflection in a classroom window. His brown eyes matched his dark blonde mop of hair, which his Mother had combed and wet down flat. She had also taken him to the mall to get his haircut yesterday. "James P. Cartwright, you have to be presentable." she had said "You don't want your hair to be as long as your sister's!"

His sister Susan was one year older, and she was a pain. She had blonde hair and blue eyes, like Mom. She was in the same school, and was always embarrassing him. Next year she would be in another school – he couldn't wait!

Susan usually hung out with her best friends Amanda Jones, Becky Petrov and Alice Wong, and steered clear of James, unless she could think of something to embarrass him. Amanda was nosy and annoying, and had long dark brown hair, green eyes and caramel-colored skin. She was a bit taller than James, and usually wasn't very nice to him. Becky and Alice were ok, for girls, they didn't say much but at least they didn't call him names like Susan or Amanda. Becky had brown wavy hair, brown eyes and freckles, and was the same height as James, though she was the same age as Amanda. Alice had black hair and dark brown eyes, and was also in his class. She sometimes shared her candies with him, and last term she was at his home group table. She sometimes smelled like strawberries.

James looked at his reflection again, messed his hair up once, twice and checked it again. Satisfied it was just messy enough, he continued walking towards his classroom.

It was an OK school, as schools went – mainly because he had some pretty cool friends in his class. Ben Jones was just the right amount of crazy, and always had big ideas. He had brown hair, brown eyes, the same caramel skin as his sister Amanda, and was a little bit taller than James. Ben was always inventing new games to play at recess and lunch, and sometimes they worked. It was fun trying out the new games, even when they didn't work out right. They usually ended up laughing and rolling on the ground anyway.

Spring Break is Over!

Games like "Elephant soccer", where you had to run around with one arm hanging down to the ground, and you had to whack the ball with your "trunk" – no using your feet. That one wasn't too bad.

"Backwards Basketball" didn't work out so well. James had run backwards over a 3rd grader and knocked him flat, giving him a bloody nose. The third grader ran crying to the office, and James got Detention. Not fair!

His other best friends were Tim & Tom O'Reilly. Tim & Tom were identical twins and sometimes completed each other's sentences. It was kind of weird, but you got used to it after a while. Otherwise they were pretty cool to hang out with. They both had curly red hair and green eyes like their Dad.

James walked slowly as he entered Miss Oliver's 5th grade classroom, yawning. He hung up his backpack on the hook under his name, crammed a bit of his recess snack into his mouth, and went over to his home group table.

He flopped down onto the chair between Tim & Tom.

"I can't believe Spring Break is over!" James mumbled through bits of Oreo crumbs.

"Yeah, I know…" said Tim

"…it's never long enough" finished Tom.

The Ultimate Tree House *Project!*

"It's gonna be like *forever* until the next holiday!" grumbled James.

Tim and Tom looked at each other, nodding.

Ben rushed into the class, full of excitement. He went to hang up his backpack on his hook, but he missed and it fell on the floor. He never noticed. He rushed over to the table where James, Tim & Tom were sitting. He was bouncing up and down.

"Hey guys, guess what I found during Spring Break?" said Ben.

"I dunno, what?" yawned James.

Just at that moment, the morning bell rang and Miss Oliver walked into the class, holding a stack of papers. She was pretty, with curly brown hair.

"Good morning children, please take your seats. I trust you had a good break and are ready to get back into school work?" she said with a smile.

All of the children groaned and Ben quickly sat down at the table.

"Oh come now, it's not that bad. Please open your workbooks to a fresh page. I have some new homework I am going to hand out now, so you have time to look at it this morning."

Spring Break is Over!

Another round of groans. Miss Oliver was a nice teacher, but for some reason she really *loved* homework.

The four friends exchanged bored glances and pulled out their books. Ben whispered "Tell you at Recess!" and quickly opened his book as Miss Oliver glanced in his direction.

James raised an eyebrow at Ben, then opened his own workbook.

At recess, James, Tim, Tom & Ben met on the side of the playground. Ben began telling them about his discovery in fast, hushed tones.

"It's completely awesome! We were doing one of those boring 'educational' family walks through the woods, you know, with Mom, Dad and Amanda – she just *had* to come along, she's like 11 but Mom says she can't stay home by herself, so she has to come with us and ruin *everything*. Anyway, Mom was telling us about the different kind of plants that we walked by, that kind of boring stuff, they all looked like weeds to me. And then – I saw it!" Ben gushed and then paused, out of breath.

The three crowded in closer to Ben.

"What was it?" said James.

"Tell us! Tell us!" cried Tim and Tom.

The Ultimate Tree House *Project!*

Ben took another breath and continued. "It was the *best*, most *awesome* tree you ever saw. It must be five times as tall as our house. And it had *huge* branches, bigger than my head! When I jumped up, I could barely reach the bottom ones. It was perfect!"

"Perfect for what?" asked James.

"For the Ultimate Tree house!" Ben replied, with a toothy grin.

James, Tim and Tom looked at each other and then back at Ben.

"It will have to be…" said Tim.

"…our secret!" finished Tom.

"No girls allowed!" insisted James.

"Especially not Amanda" agreed Ben.

"We need to check out this tree right after school!" said James.

"It's really big. We could have three or maybe even five levels!" said Ben.

"With secret entrances!" whispered Tim.

"And rope ladders and a spyglass and a flag and…" began James.

"A secret place for our comics!" interrupted Tim.

Spring Break is Over!

"What are you boys talking about?" asked Amanda, who had walked up behind the four boys while they were talking.

"Nothing!" said Ben. "Boy stuff. You wouldn't be interested. Go away, Amanda!"

"Sounds like you were talking about that big tree we saw on the walk last week with Mom & Dad" said Amanda. "What are you planning?"

"Nothing!" insisted Ben.

"It's a Secret!" muttered James.

"Oooooh, a *Secret*! I'm going to find out what it is!" she laughed as she ran off towards her friends.

"We'll have to be more careful." said Ben.

"And talk…" said Tim

"…more quietly!" agreed Tom.

2. The Tree

The boys were all watching the clock on the wall during the last lesson of the day. It moved by very, very slowly. James almost got in trouble when the teacher called his name.

"Hum, what, Miss Oliver?" he asked.

"I said, what is the capitol of Argentina?" Miss Oliver asked.

James scratched his head. He had no idea, as he had not been listening at all. "Um is it..."

Just then the bell rang. Saved by the bell! He turned in his seat, ready to go.

Miss Oliver called out to the class as they got up from their seats. "Don't forget to read chapter six! There will be a quiz on Friday."

The Tree

James grabbed his bag off the hook and headed out the door, where Ben was already waiting by the concrete step. Tim and Tom soon followed out of the classroom, swinging their bags over their shoulders at the same time. Weird.

The four friends crunched through the gravel of the schoolyard and crossed the street to the park. They walked over to the edge of the forest closest to the school. Ben looked all around and then quickly signaled them to enter the forest. They pushed through branches and stepped over tall roots that were sticking out of the ground, trying to trip them. A jungle!

The tree was only about a hundred steps in from the edge of the forest, but it was hidden from view of most of the park by a row of bushes and smaller trees. It had thick branches that spread out from the trunk at regular distances, running parallel to the ground and had large gaps in between each layer of branches. It looked like there was enough room for them to stand upright. There were a lot of branches on each level, too – plenty of support for putting boards across to start a tree house.

"It is huge!" said James.

"The branches look empty – I'll bet no-one has built in it before!" commented Ben.

"We will be the first ones!" said Tim.

"And no girls allowed!" said Tom.

They walked around the base of the tree, examining the trunk and taking turns jumping up to try and touch the lowest branches. It would not be too easy for anyone to get up, which was good. They would need a rope ladder for sure.

They all agreed the tree would be perfect for building a tree house.

"No, the *Ultimate Tree House*." said Ben.

Reluctantly, they left the tree and headed off in different directions, going home to finish their homework before dinner. Tomorrow they would start planning how to build the tree house.

At dinner, Ben's Mother asked how his first day back at school went as she served the peas.

"Fihhne" mumbled Ben through a mouth of mashed potatoes.

"Ben was talking about that tree we found," said Amanda.

"Oh really?" nodded Ben's Father. "What about the tree?"

"Nothing," muttered Ben.

The Tree

"Where did you go with your friends right after school?" asked Amanda.

"Nowhere! Just walking…just leave me alone, ok?" muttered Ben.

"Ben's got a *secret…*" started Amanda.

Ben glared at her, trying to burn a hole in her head with his eyes. She pretended to ignore him and resumed cutting her sausage.

Sisters are such a pain, thought Ben. *At least she won't be allowed in the Tree house!*

That night, Ben began to imagine the fantastic tree house that he and his friends would build. *Four, no five levels, a secret lab, a comic room, a snack room, a bowling alley, trap doors… It will be the best tree house ever!* he thought, as he finally drifted off to sleep.

3. The Sky's The Limit!

The next morning the four friends arrived early at school. James ran past the playground in the park, not even bothering to test the swing. He had more important things to do! He looked both ways at the road by the park and ran across the street. When he entered the school yard, he sprinted through the gravel, spraying rocks behind him.

Tim, Tom & Ben were waiting outside the classroom. Together, they walked over to the side of the playground where they would not be overheard.

"It's gonna be the most awesome tree house!" said James.

"What should it look like?" asked Tim.

"The sky's the limit!" replied Ben. "We can build anything we want. We have lots of wood

15

at our house, 'cos Dad just tore down the old back fence and put up a new one. Enough to build a castle!"

"We have plenty of nails and some hammers," offered James.

"We've got some rope and a couple of saws," said Tom.

"Don't you want to draw a plan or something?" asked Tim.

"Nah, we'll just make up the design as we go," said Ben. "It's better that way."

Tim looked uncertain but decided not to say anything more.

"We can start after school!" said James.

"We can meet at my house," said Ben, "and carry over some of the boards to get started. Tom, you and Tim bring the ropes so we can start on the rope ladder."

They kept talking about how great the tree house was going to be until the bell rang. They quickly headed over to Miss Oliver's class to get there before the second bell. Nobody wanted detention today!

The Ultimate Tree House *Project!*

After school, the kids each ran off toward their homes. James' house was right across the road from the park, and he gave the swing a playful tug as he went past. No time for swings today!

He entered through the side garage door and pulled off his shoes without untying them. His Mom kept telling him "untie your shoes, you are going to ruin them!" He didn't care – they still had most of their shininess and he figured stretching them would help break them in.

He ran into the kitchen to grab a quick snack before he headed to the tree. Tree house building was going to be hard work, and he needed some energy!

His Mom greeted him in the kitchen. "How was your day, honey?" she asked.

"Great! Well, school was ok I guess," replied James as he opened the pantry door. He pulled out a plastic container full of blueberry muffins and unclipped the lid. He selected one, crammed it halfway into his mouth and closed the lid. He put the container back on the shelf and closed the door.

"Learn anything?" asked his Mom.

"Nyuuhuhh" mumbled James through a mouthful of muffin. He swallowed and added "I'm going to play with Tim, Tom & Ben for a while, ok?"

The Sky's The Limit!

"That's fine. Be back before dinner, and remember you have to do your homework before bed," said his Mom.

"Yes Mom!" called James over his shoulder as he ran down the hall to the garage. He rummaged around in the cupboard beside his Dad's workbench until he found what he was looking for.

There were five bags of brand new nails sitting on the middle shelf. James grabbed one of the heavy bags and stuffed it into his pocket. He slipped his feet back into his already-tied shoes and headed out the door towards Ben's house, which was on the same street and five doors down.

When he arrived at Ben's house, his friends were waiting for him. They all went round the back to where the wood was piled up.

"Dad said we can take any of the wood we want!" said Ben, as he picked up one of the top boards. "He said the old nails have either been pulled out or bashed in, so they are safe for us to use."

There were different sizes of boards resting in neat piles – long, thick ones that used to be the fence posts, long skinny ones that used to be the top and bottom rails, and several stacks of wide, thin boards that were slightly taller than James. Those ones were the old fence slats.

"Awesome!" cried Tim.

"We can build a huge tree house with all this stuff!" agreed Tom.

"Did you bring the rope?" asked Ben.

"Sure did!" said Tim. He pulled a jumbled mass of thin rope out of his jacket.

"Dad said we could have it but we need to untangle it ourselves," said Tom.

"I've got the nails!" said James, and pulled the heavy bag out of his pocket. "But I forgot the hammer."

"We're ready to go!" said Ben. "Everyone grab some boards and we'll start taking them over to the tree."

They tried picking up the old fence posts, but they were very heavy. Tim and Tom picked up one of the old fence rails at each end, while Ben and James went to one of the slat piles and picked up three of them at once, one boy at each end. They left the backyard, went through the gate and checked both ways before crossing the street.

They carried the boards to the end of the park and stopped. Ben looked around carefully to make sure no one was watching, and then he signaled for them to go into the forest. They didn't want anyone finding their tree!

By the time they reached the tree, all four boys were getting tired. The bag of nails was poking James in the stomach.

"My hands hurt!" whined Tim.

"I think I have a splinter," moaned James.

"These boards are heavy!" groaned Tom.

"Stop complaining," growled Ben, "or we'll never start building the tree house!"

They dropped the boards under the tree with a thump, narrowly missing Tom's foot. James placed the bag of nails on the ground beside the tree. No point in carrying that heavy bag back again!

Tim dropped the tangle of thin rope beside the nails.

They returned to Ben's house for another load. They managed two more deliveries of boards to the tree before Ben's mother called him in for dinner.

James could hear his mother calling him.

"Cripes, I've got to go!" cried James.

"Us too!" echoed Tim & Tom. They lived just around the corner.

"See you all tomorrow!" yelled Ben as he disappeared inside.

James ran home with a smile on his face. *This was going to be awesome!*

The Sky's The Limit!

4. Ready, Set, Build!

The next day, the four boys spent all of recess and lunch time on the far side of the playground, talking about the tree house. Each boy had a different idea of what they should have in it, and what they should build first.

"The comic room!" cried Ben.

"We need a trapdoor first!" insisted James.

"We need a watch tower so we can watch out for anyone coming!" declared Tom.

Tim opened his mouth to speak. "I think…"

"What are you boys yelling about?" inquired Susan. She, Amanda, Becky and Alice had come up quietly behind the four boys while they were in the middle of their argument.

The four boys fell silent.

23

Ready, Set, Build!

"Aw, c'mon, it must be important." teased Alice.

"I'll bet it's about their *secret*" smirked Amanda.

"Tell us!" said Susan.

Becky stood quietly behind her friends, looking at James.

"None of your business!" said James.

"Boy stuff!" muttered Ben.

"Not for girls!" echoed Tim and Tom together.

"Humph!" grunted Susan.

"We'll see about that!" declared Alice.

"We'll find out your *secret*, you know!" Amanda laughed as the four girls walked back to the middle of the playground.

"Girls!" muttered Ben.

"Yeah…" said Tim.

"…Girls." Said Tom.

James just watched the girls as they walked away. He wasn't sure, but he thought he saw Becky give him a little smile before she turned away.

What did that mean?

The Ultimate Tree House *Project!*

After school, each of the boys ran home to get their tools and met up at Ben's house.

"I remembered the hammer!" said James.

"I brought a saw!" said Tom.

"I brought some paper and a pencil!" said Tim.

The other boys turned to look at him. "What for?" said Ben.

Tim shuffled uncertainly. "...um, to draw some plans?"

"We don't need them!" declared Ben.

"Boys build!" declared James.

"Men of action!" crowed Tom.

Tim crumpled up the paper in his pocket.

The boys went to the wood piles to pick up a few more boards to take to the tree.

"Just the railing boards this time." said Ben.

Tom balanced the saw on top of his board so he could get a good grip. James tucked the hammer inside his jacket before lifting his board.

"Let's go!" said Ben, and the boys each picked up an end of their boards and began walking to the tree.

Ready, Set, Build!

When the boys dropped their boards under the tree, Ben declared they were ready to start building. "First things first! We need to get someone up into the tree, so the rest of us can pass the boards up."

Tim and Tom exchanged glances. "We can't reach the branches." said Tom.

"Let's try climbing the trunk then!" said Ben. "James, you go try it."

James walked over to the large trunk and tried to find a handhold. The trunk was smooth and a bit slippery. From the ground all the way up past James' head, there were no knots or boles for him to get a hand or foot into or onto. He jumped up, trying to grab the bark higher up. His hands slipped off.

"I can't do it!" cried James. "It's too slippery!"

"We should have planned this better…" Tim whispered quietly to himself.

"What's that?" asked Ben, giving Tim a sharp look.

"Nothing," said Tim, "I was just thinking, if we can't climb and can't jump, we will have to wait until we grow taller to get up there."

"Brilliant idea!" said Ben. "Tim, Tom, one of you get on the other's shoulders. You should be able to reach then."

Tim bent down and Tom climbed up onto his shoulders. Tim tried to stand up. "You're heavy! Stop wiggling!"

Tom tried to hold still as Tim struggled to his feet.

"I think I can reach it!" said Tom. "Move closer to that branch over there."

Tim walked closer to the branch, Tom balancing on his shoulders. It was now at chest height for Tom. Tom grabbed onto the branch with both hands and heaved himself up onto it. Tim was relieved that the weight was gone from his shoulders. He wiggled them round and round to loosen his muscles.

"Pass me up a board!" said Tom.

Ben and James grabbed a fence slat and slid it up over the edge of the branch. Tom grabbed the edge of it and slid it up the rest of the way. He pushed the far edge of it up over the next branch, so that both ends of the board were sticking out over the two branches.

Success! Their tree house had now begun to take shape.

"Another one!" said Tom. Ben and James grabbed another board and passed it up to

Ready, Set, Build!

Tom, then another and another. Soon Tom had four fence panels straddling the two branches, and crawled over onto the new platform.

Tom stood up. "I'm the king of the world!" he shouted.

Ben and James were jumping excitedly. "My turn! My turn!" they shouted together.

Tom lay down across the boards and held his arms down. Ben grabbed onto Tom's hands but Tom was not strong enough to pull Ben up by himself.

"Tim! Get down on the ground so I can get onto your shoulders." commanded Ben.

Tim shook his head. He was still sore.

"Okay then, James, you get down on the ground and I'll get up on yours."

James did not look happy, but stooped down low so Ben could get up on his shoulders. He stood up with difficulty and walked over to the branch. Ben pulled himself up while Tom steadied him. As Ben settled onto the improvised platform, the boards shifted.

"We need to nail these down so they don't move." said Ben. "James, pass me up some nails and the hammer."

"But it's *my* hammer!" protested James.

"But *I'm* up in the tree. It won't be safe for you to climb up here too until we put some nails in these boards to stop them from moving." said Ben.

Reluctantly, James passed up the hammer, and then the bag of nails into the waiting hands of Ben and Tom.

Tim just watched, rubbing his shoulders.

After a lot of banging and one bruised thumb, Ben declared the boards were safe. "They aren't going to move. Not even a tornado would move these boards!"

"C'mon, Tom, get with me on this side of the platform and we can pull up James and Tim one at a time," commanded Ben.

Tom and Ben both lay down on the platform and reached down with one arm. Each grabbed one of James' arms and together they heaved him up onto the platform, scraping his stomach in the process.

"You next!" said Ben to Tim.

Tim stretched up both of his arms and Tom and James pulled him up onto the platform.

Proudly, the four stood on the platform and smiled at each other.

"Cahooooooooo!" crowed Tom.

"Yaheeeeee!" cried James.

Ready, Set, Build!

"King of the woooooooorld!" yelled Ben.

"I think I heard a board cracking." said Tim, with a worried look on his face.

"Ok, now we need to make it easier to get up for next time." said Ben. "Who brought the rope up?"

Tim and Tom looked at each other and then down at the base of the tree. The tangle of rope was still on the ground.

"Darn it!" said Ben. "Why didn't you bring it up with you?"

"You didn't tell me to." Said Tim.

"I got up here first, not my fault!" said Tom.

"Not my rope!" said James.

Together they stood and looked down at the rope.

"You know what we need?" said Ben.

"…better planning?" said Tim.

Ben glared at him and turned away. "We need a leader. And I'm it!"

Tom and James looked at each other and shrugged. Tim rolled his eyes. What a surprise – *not*!

The Ultimate Tree House *Project!*

In the distance they heard Ben's mother calling him in for dinner.

"Cripes! It's late!" said James.

"See you all tomorrow!" yelled Ben, as he jumped down out of the tree and ran towards home, not waiting for his friends.

James hung his feet over the edge and dropped to the ground. The landing made his feet sting. He helped Tom and Tim jump down to the ground by steadying them as they landed. The three friends walked out of the darkening forest together and then ran to the edge of the park. They walked across the street just as the first street light turned on. The walked together in silence until Tim & Tom turned right down the street that led to their house.

"See you tomorrow!" yelled James as they walked away.

"See you…" said Tim.

"…Tomorrow!" said Tom.

Ready, Set, Build!

5. Disaster!

The next day after school, the boys met at Ben's house.

"As your leader," declared Ben, "our priority is to get the rope ladder sorted out so it is easier for us to get up every day."

Ben looked around at the other boys.

"So…anyone know how to make a rope ladder?" Ben asked.

The other three boys exchanged glances and shook their heads.

"I've seen one on TV." said Tom.

"Me too!" said James.

"Oh boy." said Tim, shaking his head again.

Disaster!

"Ok, so much for that idea. But it can't be that hard. We'll figure it out, boys are *smart*!" announced Ben.

Amanda was watching them from her bedroom window upstairs, peeking from behind the curtain. The window was open and she could hear the boys quite clearly.

"…we had better get started then." continued Ben. "Off to the tree house, but make sure nobody is watching when we go into the forest!"

So that is where they are going, thought Amanda. *I should have guessed.*

The boys headed off through the park, tools in hand. One of them was whistling but from where she was watching, Amanda could not tell who it was. She waited for another thirty seconds and then left the house. She hid around the corner, watching the boys until they disappeared into the forest. *So that is where it is!* she thought to herself.

She walked quickly across the quiet road and through the park to the edge of the forest. *They went in somewhere around here, looked like they were heading straight in*, she thought. She pulled her Girl Guide compass out of her pocket and looked in the direction she saw the boys enter the forest. She lined up the red compass arrow pointing north, then squinted along the line of the compass in the direction

The Ultimate Tree House *Project!*

she thought they went. *Gotcha*! She thought as she slowly walked into the forest, carefully making her way through the bushes and trees, all the while watching the direction on the compass.

When she arrived at the tree, the boys were arguing and did not notice her at first.

"I get to go up first!" said James.

"I'm the leader!" insisted Ben. "I get to go up first!"

"I am better at getting up than any of you, I did it first last time!" said Tom.

Tim watched the three argue and then looked up at the platform. *Boards look pretty thin*, he thought.

He heard a twig snap behind him and turned.

Surprise filled his face. "Girl Alert!" he yelled.

At once, the other three boys stopped arguing and turned to face Tim and Amanda.

"What are you doing here?" demanded Ben.

"Just going for a walk." said Amanda.

"A likely story. You followed us!" yelled Ben, getting angry.

35

Disaster!

"Did not! It's a free forest, you know!" Amanda yelled back.

"No girls allowed!" said James.

"Go home!" said Ben.

"No, you can't make me." Amanda stubbornly replied.

"Don't you come any closer or I'll…" started Ben.

"You'll what?" asked Amanda, stretching up to her full height, reminding Ben who was the bigger sibling.

You can't hit girls, and besides she would just tell Mom… thought Ben. "Aww nuts. We'll just have to pretend she's not here." he muttered to the other boys.

The boys slowly turned and went back to their tree house building.

Amanda stood and watched the boys for a while, then settled herself on the ground, leaning back against a smaller tree trunk facing the big tree.

She watched Ben and James struggle to get up onto the platform, while Tim and Tom tried to unravel the rope. *Hopeless*, she thought, *completely hopeless*.

Eventually they got the rope untangled and stretched it out on the ground.

"So, now how do we make the rope ladder?" asked Tom.

"Throw one end up over the branch." commanded Ben.

Tom threw one end up over the branch.

"Now James, you tie it to the branch" he called up to James, who had been the "winner of who gets to go up first". James insisted he had earned it from getting the scratches on his stomach from being pulled up yesterday. "Battle-scars," he called them.

"I don't know how to tie a knot!" James called back down to Ben.

Amanda smiled. "I know how to..." she started to say, but was interrupted by Ben.

"No girls here!" he declared.

"But I *know...*" she started again.

"No! We don't need you here! Go away!" shouted Ben.

Frustrated, Amanda got up and turned to walk home.

"But I know how to do it!" she called out, then stormed off through the woods towards home.

"**No Girls Allowed!**" chorused all of the boys as she left.

Disaster!

BOYS! She thought to herself, fuming all the way home. *BOYS!*

"This is a DISASTER," declared Ben. "She knows our secret and she is going to ruin *everything*!"

6. This Means War!

When Amanda got home, she went into the kitchen to talk to her Mom. Instead, she found her father getting a drink of water from the tap.

"Where's Mom?" asked Amanda.

"She just went to the store to pick up some spices for dinner. We ran out." Her father said. "What's up, kiddo? You look upset."

"Boys are stupid." she said.

Her father raised his eyebrows. "All boys? Including me?"

Amanda looked at her father. *Oops!* "No, of course not YOU, Dad. You know, BOYS. Especially Ben."

"Oooh, *Boys*. What seems to be the problem?" asked her father in a gentle tone.

This Means War!

"They just, they just….ooooo! They are so *annoying* sometimes!" she exclaimed. "I know how to do what they need to do and they won't let me help them because I'm a *GIRL*."

"And what do they need to do?" he inquired.

"Build a tree house. I mean, the rope ladder for it. I know how to make one, I learned it in Girl Guides. But they won't listen. They are just dumb boys. They said that *No Girls were Allowed*, and that's not fair!" she pouted.

"Well, what's stopping you from building your own tree house?" asked her father, looking at her closely.

"I….what?" she stopped and looked at her father. "What do you mean?"

"Well, you seem to know how to do some of the things that these *silly boys* don't know how to do, so why don't you build your own tree house?" He looked at her with a sly smile on his face. "We have lots of wood left in the yard from the old fence, and you are welcome to use it to build your own tree house too."

Realization of what her father was saying crept across her face like a sunrise. "Really? Can I? I mean us Girls? Can we?" she blurted out.

"Of course. Girls are just as capable as boys. Plus you will have a secret weapon!" he announced.

"What secret weapon?" she asked.

"Me!" said her Dad.

"Huh?" she looked at her father closely. "What do you mean?"

"Do you want to make a tree house like your brother?" asked her father.

"Yes! I mean no, the boys' one looks silly. I want to build a *better* tree house than them." She crossed her arms and raised her head defiantly. "I want to build a *much better* tree house than *Ben and his gang.*"

"Oh really?" smiled her Dad. "Are you willing to pay the price?"

Amanda suddenly looked uncertain. "What price? I don't have much of my allowance left. It's not Saturday yet."

Her Dad smiled. "Not your money, Amanda. You keep that. The price I am talking about is taking the time to *learn how to build your tree house the right way.*"

"And what is the right way?" asked Amanda, now puzzled.

"As a PROJECT." declared her Dad.

This Means War!

"Awww Dad, not *work stuff*!" groaned Amanda. Her father was a Project Manager for a local construction company. "Work stuff is *boring*!"

"Just wait and listen," continued her father. "You need a bit of this *work stuff* in order to make your tree house better than Ben's."

He paused, noting his daughter's scowl. "Not only am I going to tell you how to make a better tree house than Ben, I am going to show you that you can do it *easier* than him. Are you interested?"

Better? Easier? she thought. She liked the idea of that. "Okay Dad, tell me how to do it!"

"Well first, Mandy, I need to draw you some pictures." her father replied. "Please go into my office and grab some blank pieces of paper and a ruler and meet me at the kitchen table."

Amanda went down the hallway and entered her father's "home office". She opened the printer tray and pulled out five pieces of blank paper. She closed the printer tray and walked back to the kitchen where her father was waiting at the table.

"Have a seat, Amanda." said her father. "No, not in your normal seat. Sit beside me so you can see what I am drawing."

Amanda moved around the table to sit beside her father.

He pulled a mechanical pencil from his shirt pocket and drew some lines using the ruler and wrote some notes.

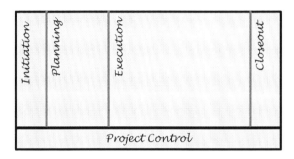

"There are four steps to every project," her father spoke in a formal voice. "Initiation, Planning, Execution and Closeout. Well, five if you count Control, which kind of happens for the whole project."

Amanda looked at the words. "Initiation? What's that? And Execution – people don't get *killed* on your projects, do they Dad?"

Her father looked at the paper thoughtfully for a moment. "Initiation is getting things started. And no, honey, we don't kill people. I think I might need to use some better words for you. Let's try something else."

He flipped the paper over, lined up the ruler and drew another diagram.

"Okay, how about this. Idea, Plan, Do and Finish Up. Sound better?" he asked.

"Much better, thanks Dad." smiled Amanda.

"And then instead of 'Control' we have 'Lead, Check and Correct'." Her father suggested.

"Ok, I guess…" Amanda wiggled in her seat. "You explain it first and I'll tell you if we need different words."

"Ok honey, that's fine. So you know what an Idea is, right?" asked her father, with a wink.

Amanda sat up straight and stuck out her tongue. "Of course I know what an *Idea* is. C'mon, Dad!"

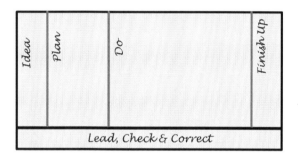

"Okay, just checking." He smiled. "And you understand what Plan is, right?"

"Like when you want to do something but you are not sure how, so you have to think about how you are going to do it?" Amanda suggested.

"Right, that's pretty close. Though at work, even when we pretty much know what we are going to do, we still take time to discuss it and see if we want to do it the same way, or if we want to try to do it a different way." Her father replied.

"And 'Do'?" her father asked, "That's an easy one too. Not too hard yet, right?"

"Not too hard, Dad. I am *Eleven* you know…" she squinted up at him.

"Right, of course, you're *Eleven*." Her father drew out the last word.

"So 'Finish Up' is pretty obvious too, huh?" asked her father.

"Yeah Dad, our teacher keeps telling us to hurry and finish up our work." She yawned. "Sorry, Dad, it's kind of boring so far. I'm not a little kid. So where is the secret weapon part?"

"Almost there, I will speed it up a little. The bottom part is important. Well, all parts are, but that part is kind of a big part of my job at work, so at least I think it is important, anyway." Her father paused and rubbed his eyes.

"Ok Dad, tell me…" she started.

"Ok, well the 'Control' part, or 'Lead, Check and Correct' as I wrote it for you, is important because it is how you make sure you are still doing what you are supposed to do – and will end up with what you wanted in the first place."

This Means War!

"Like when we do a quiz at school and the teacher tells us to check over our answers before we hand it in?" asked Amanda.

"Kind of like that, yes." said her father.

"Ok Dad, that's great. Thanks!" Amanda started to get up from the table.

"Hold on honey, there is a little bit more for tonight. I need to explain some more before we have dinner." Her father motioned for Amanda to sit.

Amanda sat down.

"Now what did you see when you were watching your brother and his friends today at the tree?" asked her father.

"They were arguing and fighting over things. They didn't seem to know what they were doing," she said. "Each one of them had ideas they were saying but the others did not seem to be listening."

"Hmmmmm," said her father. "I think this might be what is going on then."

He pulled out a fresh piece of paper and drew another picture.

"I think they went straight from 'Idea' to 'Do'" mused her father. "That's usually a recipe for disaster."

"They weren't cooking, Dad. They were trying to build a tree house." corrected Amanda.

"Yes, dear, you are right. What I mean is, it sounds like they skipped Planning and jumped right into Doing. I see people try to do that a lot, and it rarely works out well. They usually fail." Her father rubbed his temples.

"Fail? Like on a test at school?" asked Amanda, with a curious look.

"Different. Fail in a way that if a person does not do their job right, people can get hurt," sighed her father. "Either that, or they waste a lot of time and money trying to do something that does not work like it is supposed to, and they have to redo things to make it work right."

"Ok Dad, you said we were almost to the 'secret weapon' part…" urged Amanda, fidgeting in her seat.

"Well if you look at the drawing of what your brother and his friends seem to be doing, there is a part we said was missing, right?" he asked.

"The Planning part, right Dad?" said Amanda.

"Right. The Planning part is the *secret weapon*. All of the parts are important, but by far that is the most important of all." Her father coughed, took a sip of water and then continued. "I am going to draw you one more picture, and that will be it for tonight. You have been studying hard."

Studying? thought Amanda, *She wasn't studying – was she?*

Her father pulled out his ruler and flipped over the paper. He set the ruler and drew another drawing:

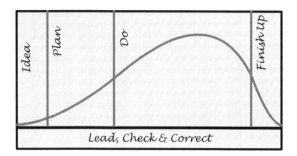

"See the curve? That shows how much time and effort you should spend in each phase of your project. The curve can be a bit different depending on your project, but notice how there is a big part of it in the Planning section?" asked her father.

"Ummm..yeah?" yawned Amanda.

"Well, that is where you need to spend a lot of your effort, *before* you start really doing things on your project." Her father watched her eyes closely. They were beginning to wander. He heard the front door open and then close. His wife was home; dinner would be ready soon.

"That's enough for today, honey. You take these drawings with you, and go work on your homework for a few minutes. Then please wash up and help your Mom, okay?" Her father smiled at her.

"Yes Dad." said Amanda. She stood up and then stretched as she walked down the hallway to her bedroom.

She has a lot to learn, he thought. *This is going to be an interesting challenge. Boys against the Girls (…and Dad!)*

This Means War!

7. Idea, Plan, What?

The next morning Amanda got up early and dressed quickly. She went into the kitchen where she found her father buttering toast at the table. He had been reading the paper and his cup of coffee was half-empty. Ben was still down the hall, lying in bed. He usually tried to sleep in as long as he could, and would even pretend to be asleep when his Mom came into his room to open the curtains and wake him up. He would probably be in bed for another fifteen minutes or so.

Amanda sat down at the table and poured some cereal into her bowl. Mom always set the table before they went to bed, "so the mornings would go quicker" she would say. Amanda shook an extra flake into her bowl before placing the box in the middle of the table. She poured the milk and put the jug down.

Idea, Plan, What?

"Good morning, Dad." said Amanda.

"Oh, good morning dear. How are you this morning? Have a good sleep?" asked her Dad, still half-reading the paper.

"Okay I guess. I had trouble getting to sleep." She replied.

"Oh really?" asked her father as he folded the paper and pushed it aside. "And why do you think that is?"

"I was thinking about the pictures you drew last night and what you said. It kind of made sense but I still don't see how just saying 'Plan' is a secret weapon. There has to be more to it, right Dad?" she looked at her father with a hopeful look in her eyes.

"Well, yes, there is a lot more to it, but what we covered last night was probably enough to start with. When you are ready, we can go into a bit more detail."

"I'm ready NOW, Dad." insisted Amanda as she popped a spoonful of cereal into her mouth and began to chew. "Imh rheady" she mumbled through the cereal.

Her father sighed. "Well, unfortunately, honey, I'm not ready. I have to go to work a bit early today, there are a few problems on my current project and I have to check in with the team to see how we can fix them. Plus, I need to think about how I am going to do our next lesson, and that needs a bit more time."

Amanda swallowed her mouthful. "Can we do it *today*, Dad?" begged Amanda. "I really want to beat Ben."

Her father sighed. "Tonight, after work. I don't know how ready I will be, but we'll give it a shot."

"Thanks Dad," smiled Amanda.

Her father got up from the table and kissed her on the forehead. "Have a good day, sweetie. Don't let Ben bug you too much."

"You too, Dad!" said Amanda, then popped another spoonful of cereal into her mouth as he headed for the garage.

Just then, Ben came out into the kitchen in his pyjamas, yawning and stretching. "What were you and Dad just talking about?" he asked.

"Nothing you would be interested in. *Girl* stuff." She said.

"Humph." Said Ben as he sat down at the table and reached for the bran flakes. He poured himself a very full bowl and then poured in the milk. Some of the flakes pushed out onto the table when he stuck his spoon into the bowl. *She's up to something*, he thought.

Idea, Plan, What?

At recess, Ben and his group of tree house builders met at their usual spot on the side of the playground.

"I don't know what it is, but Amanda is planning something," muttered Ben. "She's probably going to do something really mean and ruin everything."

After Amanda had left the tree the prior afternoon, all four boys had begun to worry. *Now that their secret tree house had been discovered, how many people would she tell?* they all wondered.

"Right, now that our tree house has been found, we need to work on our defenses," said Ben.

"Why don't we forget the rope ladder idea, it would only make it easier for someone to get up," suggested Tom.

"Good idea," added Tim. *We don't know how to make one yet anyway*, he thought to himself.

James lifted his shirt and examined the new batch of scratches on his stomach from being pulled up onto the platform yesterday. "I don't know…" he mused. "It might be handy to have one. Maybe we could hide it up on the platform so nobody can reach it."

"Your sister is taller than you, dummy," exclaimed Ben. "No rope ladder. We do it the hard way. We're tough! We're boys!"

Reluctantly, the other boys agreed with Ben. *They couldn't make it too easy for the enemy!*

The bell rang and children started running from the playground toward their classrooms.

"We'll start building our defenses after school." decided Ben, as they walked back to Miss Oliver's class.

After school, Amanda did her best to ignore the sounds of the boys talking outside. They were picking up another load of wood and taking it over to the tree house. She turned up the music on her MP3 player a little bit louder and adjusted the headphones to cover her ears better. Eventually the sound of the boys disappeared off in the direction of the park. She turned down the music again and tried to concentrate on her homework, so that she could have it finished before her father got home. She had a lot of questions for him.

Finally, she heard the garage door open and a car pull in. She hopped up off her bed, and walked into the kitchen. She already had a

Idea, Plan, What?

small stack of blank paper and the ruler ready and waiting, with the drawings from last night placed neatly beside the blank paper.

Her father came in from the hallway, looking tired.

"Hard day, Dad?" inquired Amanda.

"You could say that." he replied. He noticed the paper and ruler on the table and then looked up into the eager eyes of his daughter. "Just give me a few minutes, honey. I need to unpack my briefcase and I think take a short nap."

Amanda was disappointed but she knew the routine. Usually when Dad came home and was extra tired from work, he would lie down on the couch for a twenty minute nap. He seemed to be okay after that, and had more energy. She couldn't figure it out – *naps were for little kids*, she thought. Anyway, whatever. She got herself a snack from the cupboard and poured herself a glass of milk. She doodled on the corner of one of the pieces of blank paper until her father came into the kitchen.

He rubbed his eyes and stretched. "That's much better!" he said. "Now I can concentrate."

He got a glass from the cupboard and filled it from the kitchen tap. He sipped the water as he sat down at the table beside Amanda.

"Okay, so what do you want to know first?" he asked.

"Everything! How to make a tree house! How to beat Ben! How to make it better than him….and beat Ben!" she declared.

"Whoa!" her father fell back in his chair. "One thing at a time. This morning you said you wanted to know more about planning – at least enough for you to build this fort thingy."

"Tree House, Dad." she corrected.

"Right, Tree House. Well, first you start with the Idea, right?" he began.

"We did that yesterday, Dad." said Amanda.

"Well, kind of. Be patient. What is the Idea?" asked her father.

"To build a Tree House. A Better Tree House." stated Amanda, matter-of-factly.

"Ok, then, you know what you want to make. To build a better Tree House than your brother. But what does it *look* like?" he asked.

"I don't know, we haven't built it yet!" she wailed, getting frustrated.

"Right, well if you don't know what it looks like, how will you build it, and if you build it, how will you know you are done?" her father took a sip of water and continued. "There is a famous saying, *If you don't know where you are going, any road will get you there*."

Amanda turned sideways to look at him. "What?"

"What I am saying," said her father, "is that you need to have a picture in your head or *Vision* of what this tree house should look like when you are done. Otherwise, you might just end up doing what Ben has been doing."

She considered that for a moment. "I don't want to do that!"

"Well, you don't have to know *exactly* how it will look when you are finished. Especially with a tree house, there will be a lot of variables…"

Amanda interrupted him. "varia-what?"

Her father apologized. "Sorry, more work language. I mean that there are a lot of things you won't know as you build something like a house in a tree. But the key here is that you should have an *Idea* of what your tree house might look like, and what your basic *requirements* are – how many levels, how many walls, doors, rope ladders, stuff like that."

"Oh, I got it. I don't have to draw it, just imagine it?" she asked.

"To start with, anyway. If you are the only one doing the work, it might be okay to just work with the picture in your head, unless you forget things easily. But if you have people helping you, it is better to draw it on paper." He yawned, shook his head and had another sip of water. "Especially when you start 'Doing' stuff, the more you have written down the better, because it makes it easier to communicate your ideas with your team."

"So you don't end up with doors upside-down, things like that?" she giggled.

"Right, or too many doors, or walls where a door should be. Or bits of the floor missing. It can get pretty messy," he said.

Amanda smiled. "Okay, Dad, so what's next?"

Her Dad pulled a piece of paper from the stack. "Let's start with the simple stuff. How many floors do you want in your Tree House?"

Amanda looked at the ceiling. "I'm not sure, it depends how big the tree is and how strong, I guess. One, or two maybe."

"Okay," said her father, "one or two floors." He made a note on the paper. "How will you get up?"

She poked out her tongue, just a little. "A rope ladder, Dad, I *told* you I know how to make one."

Idea, Plan, What?

"Okay then, one rope ladder." He wrote that down too. "So what do you think you might need to build your Tree House?"

"Well, some wood...and rope for the rope ladder and some nails." she said.

Her father wrote that down too, but in a different spot on the paper. "What tools do you think you might need?"

"A hammer, a saw, and it might be easier to make the rope ladder if I could make some holes for the rope to go through the boards. Hey, can I borrow your drill, Dad?" she asked.

"Yes, you can honey, but I need to make sure you know how to use it safely first. And you will have to use it at home."

Amanda knew her father looked after his tools, so she said "But Dad, I will take good care of it. Can I bring it to the tree?"

Her father smiled and said "It probably won't work in the forest, unless your tree is next to a current bush."

"What's that?" she looked puzzled.

"Bad joke" said her father. I mean it's a long way from our house and my extension cords are not very long."

"Oh. Right." she said. "Okay I can make the holes here I guess."

The Ultimate Tree House *Project!*

"I have a couple more important questions for you." said her father. "1. Don't you think you need someone to help you? and 2. Which tree are you going to build in?"

"Well, I thought my friends could help me build it, you know, Susan, Becky and Alice." she looked thoughtful.

"...and the tree?" asked her father.

"Oh, um, I don't know yet. We will have to look I guess. As faaaar away from Ben as possible, I think." she scowled. "I don't want him near our tree house. He stinks!"

"One more question. Do you know when you might want to have this tree house finished?" he asked.

"By the end of school, if we can. It would be nice to play in it for the summer," she replied.

"Okay, that is your *target deadline* – when you want the project to be finished."

Her father made some more notes on the paper and then showed it to Amanda.

Tree House Requirements
- *1 or 2 levels*
- *Rope ladder*
- *Far from boys*

Target Deadline
- *Finish by Summer* *

Idea, Plan, What?

Resources

- *Rope*
- *Wood*
- *Nails*
- *Hammer*
- *Saw*
- *Drill*

Team

- *Susan*
- *Becky*
- *Alice*
- *Amanda*

Skills Needed

- *Tie Knots*
- *Measure*
- *Saw Boards*
- *Drill Holes*
- *Safety First!*

"These are your basic *requirements* over here, some of the *resources* you are going to need to get for the project, and some of the *skills* for the *tasks* you are going to need to do." said her father as he pointed to each section of the paper.

"Now, I am going to draw a picture with some of the items on this paper, but in a different way." her father moved the first piece of paper aside and began to draw on the fresh piece of paper.

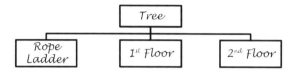

"Here is a picture that shows **what** you want to get done - what you want to build. And under the top one are some of the things you will need to build or complete in order to make it happen." He added to the diagram.

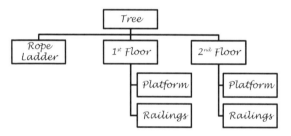

"You can add more and more details, like the platform and the railings for each level, because you will build those as part of each level." He wrote down the another list of items on the paper.

Tasks
- *Find Tree*
  - *Search forest*
  - *Check size and branches*
  - *Select tree*
- *Make Rope Ladder*

Idea, Plan, What?

- ○ *Measure height*
- ○ *Drill holes*
- ○ *Anchor ropes to tree (tie knots)*
- ○ *Fit rungs onto ropes*
- ○ *Tie knots*
- *Build Level 1*
  - ○ *Test branches*
  - ○ *Measure boards*
  - ○ *Fasten boards*
  - ○ *Add railings*
- *Build Level 2*
  - ○ *Test branches*
  - ○ *Measure boards*
  - ○ *Fit boards*
  - ○ *Fasten boards*
  - ○ *Add railings*
  - ○ *etc*

"These are some of the things you need to do - we call them *tasks*. When you finish each task, it helps you make progress towards your goal of building your tree house."

"Ok, thanks Dad! I can get started now!" she moved to get up.

"Wait a second, Mandy. First things first. Actually that is a good way to say what I was going to show you next." He paused and drew again.

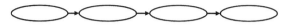

Her father had drawn a number of little bubbles, in a row.

"First things first means that you need to do some things and finish them before you do the next one. When this happens we call it a *dependency*, and it helps us to define our *sequence*." her father took another sip of water and placed the glass back on the table.

He drew another set of bubbles.

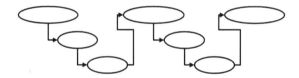

"The bigger bubbles can be broken down into smaller ones, which come from our tasks. For example, building level 1 depends on the last part of the rope ladder being finished, and you have to finish the steps for Level 1 before you can start to build Level 2. Level 1 is *dependent* on the Rope Ladder, and Level 2 is *dependent* on Level 1."

"Dad, this is getting too complicated."

"Really? well let's try a different example. When you have dinner tonight, will you eat the food before it is cooked?"

"Of course not, Dad, unless we only have a salad."

Idea, Plan, What?

"Will you wash your hands before dinner?"

"You and Mom say you won't let us eat until we have washed our hands..."

"Do you have dessert before dinner?"

Amanda's eyes brightened. "Can we, Dad? Can we?"

"No, honey, not going to happen. But you see that there is often a logical order to things, a way that makes more sense than other ways, like it just fits together?"

Amanda got a sly look. "Dessert before dinner kind of makes sense, Dad..."

"Nice try." he smiled.

Amanda pouted. "Awww Dad, pleeeease..."

He shook his head.

"Now I want you to help me with this part. Which is the most important thing to do first?"

"Ummm... Rope ladder?" she guessed.

"What about find a tree first?"

Oh duh.... She thought. "Okay okay. We find the tree and *then* make the rope ladder, so we can get up. That will make it easier to build it."

"Just build the rope ladder? How long does it need to be? How much rope do you need?" he asked.

"I don't know yet. Long enough to reach the ground."

"and that is...?"

Amanda was getting frustrated. "I won't know until we find the tree!"

"Are you starting to see how this works?"

"Yes Dad. It seems like a lot of work. No wonder Ben just started to build." she slumped back in her seat.

"Yes, it is a lot of work," agreed her father.

He drew more bubbles and filled them in, drawing a line through one of them. "When you draw your tasks like this, it makes it easier to see what needs to be done, and in what order. If you know when you want to be finished, it helps to figure out how long you have to finish each task when you plan them. If some tasks take too long, you will know that either you will not finish on time, or you will have to make some changes to your plan."

"So how is all of this a secret weapon?" she whined.

Idea, Plan, What?

"Ah... the secret is the more you plan up front, the easier it is to do the project. You make fewer mistakes and rework, have less frustration and are more likely to end up with what you wanted in the first place." he smiled.

"Dad, I don't know if I want to build a tree house any more. It sounds too hard now."

"Well, that is up to you honey. If you don't want to build one, then don't. But on the other hand..." he paused.

"What?" she asked.

"...Ben will have a tree house and you won't. Ben will win. I wasn't going to tell you yet but there is one more secret weapon."

"Dad...."

"Really, this one is super powerful." He smiled.

Amanda sighed. "Okay Dad, tell me..."

"You will always do better if you have a good *Team*."

Amanda was getting hungry. "Uh-huh. Almost done, Dad?"

"Yes dear. I am going to sum up what we covered today in a few simple phrases." He began to write.

- *What do you want to have at the end?*
- *Can you break it into parts?*

- When do you want to be finished?

- What tasks (actions) do you need to do?

- What tools and materials and people do you need so you can do the tasks?

- Which tasks have to be done before other ones?

Amanda yawned. "Are we done *now* Dad?"

"Yes. Enough for now. Take the papers with you. You might want them later."

"Uh-huh." she grunted and got up. She took the papers to her bedroom and tossed them on her dresser.

Building a tree house is no fun if you have to do all this work stuff, she thought. *Let Ben build his silly tree house, see if I care!*

Idea, Plan, What?

8. The Plan

The next morning at recess Amanda saw the boys talking as usual on the side of the playground. She ignored them and walked over to where Susan, Becky and Alice were waiting by the swings.

"Boys are stupid!" exclaimed Amanda.

"Of course! All boys are stupid," agreed Susan. "Especially brothers."

Becky looked across the playground at James and his friends. "All boys? Maybe not all boys."

"Well those four for sure." said Amanda.

Alice pushed her left toe into the gravel. "What has Ben done this time?"

"Building a dumb tree house. I found them working on it two days ago. They were arguing

71

about how to build a rope ladder. I tried to help them but they told me to go away. They are so annoying!" fumed Amanda.

"So?" asked Becky.

"So remember last fall at camp? We learned how to make one in Girl Guides." replied Amanda. "But the boys wouldn't let me help because I'm a Girl."

The other three looked at each other and nodded. "Boys!"

"I told my Dad about it and he said, why don't you girls build your own tree house?" continued Amanda. "He said he had a *secret weapon* so we could build ours better and easier than the boys."

Curious, Alice asked "So what did he say? What was the secret weapon?"

"Dad said it was *planning*. Like his work. He drew me some pictures and stuff. But it was getting too hard. He said it was going to be *easier* but then said we have to do all this other stuff first. It is going to take forever Dad's way!" frowned Amanda.

"So what are you going to do?" asked Alice.

"I dunno. I told Dad it was too hard but he said then Ben will *win*!"

The Ultimate Tree House *Project!*

Susan spoke up. "We are smarter than those silly boys. We can make a tree house way better than they could, especially better than our little brothers!"

"I'll help!" said Becky.

"Me too!" said Alice.

"We will all come over to your house after school," announced Susan. "We will figure it out together and make a *way* better tree house than those boys!"

After school, the girls met at Amanda's house. She invited them in and they went into the kitchen.

"Help yourself to some cookies" said her mother. "I just baked them today. Milk is in the fridge."

"Mmmmm, chocolate chip!" smiled Alice. "Thanks, Mrs. Jones!"

A chorus of "Thanks!" and "Mmmmm good!" followed from the girls.

Once they had finished eating, Susan spoke to Amanda. "So where are these drawings and stuff your Dad did?"

"In my bedroom. I'll go get them," said Amanda.

The Plan

She came back with the drawings, some blank paper and a pencil. The girls all sat down at the table.

"Okay," said Susan, "Show us what your Dad taught you."

Amanda showed the other girls each page and explained what she could remember.

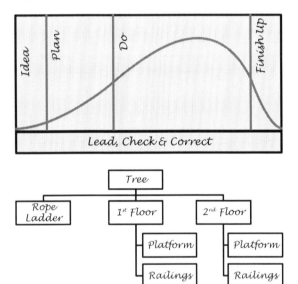

"Okay, let me see if I've got it," said Susan. "Idea, Plan, Do, Finish Up. Figure out what you want to do, and break that down into smaller pieces that fit together. Then figure out which ones have to happen before other ones, and what stuff you need to do it. Then do it!"

"Well, yeah…" said Amanda.

The Ultimate Tree House *Project!*

"So what's so hard about that?" asked Susan, raising an eyebrow.

"It's not hard to understand, it was all the stuff that I needed to do to make it work that was hard!" Amanda pouted.

Becky sniffed. "Doesn't sound that hard."

Alice agreed. "We could do all that stuff, easy."

Susan added "We can do it *together*. What did your Dad say the other secret weapon was? A good Team? Us Girl Guides stick together, you know!"

"Okay, I guess we can. I really don't want Ben to win." Amanda frowned.

"Okay then. Let's use your Dad's pictures as a start and draw our own. We'll even make it better – 'cos we *Girls* are doing it!" smiled Becky.

The girls spread out the papers on the table and then started drawing and making notes. Pretty soon, Amanda had to go into her father's office and "borrow" some more blank paper from the printer.

A short time later, Amanda's father arrived home to find the four girls all talking excitedly, writing and drawing at the kitchen table.

"What are you girls up to?" he asked.

"Building a Tree House!" they all chorused.

The Plan

As her father turned to head into the living room, a small smile crept onto his face.

At dinner time, Ben sat down at the table with a smirk on his face. Amanda looked at him and his smirk grew even bigger.

"What are you up to, Ben?" she asked.

"Nothing, boy stuff...but you'll see if you ever come to our tree again," he smiled.

"We don't care about your silly tree house. Us *Girls* are going to build our own, and it's gonna be waaay better than yours!" she declared.

"Betcha can't!" replied Ben.

"We can! We will!" her voice was getting louder.

"Kids! Kids! Simmer down!" said their father, a stern expression on his face. "No fighting at the table."

Ben and Amanda glared at each other but stopped talking.

"We *can*, and we *will*," muttered Amanda under her breath.

After dinner, Amanda showered first, then came out in to the living room in her pyjamas. Ben had already gone into the bathroom to have his shower, poking his tongue out at her as he went by.

"Um Dad..." started Amanda.

"Yes, honey?" came a voice from behind the newspaper.

"Can I show you the planning stuff we did after school? I want to make sure we are doing it right. Once we started working on it, it seemed kind of simple, so I want to check with you." Amanda brought her right hand in front of her. She was holding some rolled up papers.

Her father closed the newspaper and put it down on the couch. "Sure, Mandy. Let's go over to the kitchen table."

"Just a quick look, Dad, I don't want Ben to see," pleaded Amanda.

"Sure thing. Let's have a look at what you have done."

Amanda spread out the papers on the table. "We used different sheets of paper. This one is the Idea, and the other one is what we have for Planning.

The Plan

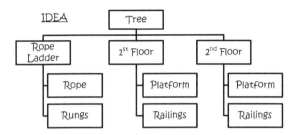

"The bubbles were getting too squishy so we moved them around," she pointed.

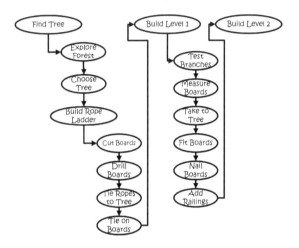

"Hmmm..." Her father looked at it all, going over each page several times. "Pretty good start."

"We also changed your other picture, Dad – we all liked '**Think-Plan-Do-Finish Up'** better than '**Idea-Plan-Do-Finish Up**', because that way they are all action words."

The Ultimate Tree House *Project!*

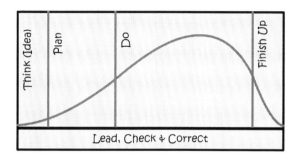

"So what do you think, Dad? Did we do it right?" asked Amanda, looking uncertain.

"Yes, you have a very good start here. I just have a few questions." He pointed to **Choose Tree**. "How will you know when you have found a good tree?"

Amanda put her finger on her lip. "I dunno, Dad. How big of a tree do we need?"

"The branches of the tree should be at least as big around as the top of your leg," he answered. "The bigger the better, but the branch should not move much at all when you hang from it with your hands. If it does, it is too small."

Amanda made a note on the paper. "Thanks Dad."

He smiled, and then pointed to **Measure Boards**. "How will you measure the boards?"

Amanda had her answer ready. "We can take a board to the tree and see if it fits between the branches?"

79

The Plan

"That's a good idea. But you need to make sure that the ends of the board stick out past the branches. You might also want to add some supports if you are trying to build a larger platform."

Her father looked over the diagrams and lists again, which had a number of additions from the lists they had drawn up the other evening.

"Very good, Mandy. This looks like a good plan. And remember, you can always add more detail as you go," smiled her father. "If you need any more help, let me know."

Amanda beamed. "Thanks Dad! We are going to start looking for a tree tomorrow. And we'll have all day to look 'cos it's Saturday!"

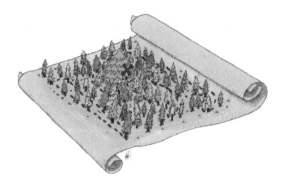

9. The Tree Hunt

The next morning the girls met at Amanda's house. They all had sturdy shoes on to go "tree hunting" as Becky called it, the same shoes they wore the last time they went camping. Each of them had a small backpack, a water bottle, wrapped lunch and a snack. Amanda had a camera, her compass, a notepad and pencil. She also had her mom's cellphone "just in case you get lost," her mother had said.

"Don't go too far, Dear!" called Amanda's mother from the top of the stairs. "Keep to the woods by the school. Remember, don't cross the creek, it's been raining and the water will be high. Stick together and be home before dinner!"

"We will, Mom!" Amanda yelled back up the stairs.

81

The Tree Hunt

The four girls crossed over into the park and walked over to the edge of the woods.

It wasn't a very large forest, really; it was the remains of a much bigger one from the days before they developed the surrounding neighborhoods and the school about thirty years ago. It had a lot of second growth trees; it was perhaps two blocks long by one block wide, the same width as the park and running along the side of the school, and it ended up down by the creek. Still, it was a big enough forest to do lots of exploring.

"Right, girls! Check your compass bearings so we keep going straight!" called out Amanda. They had planned to check the whole forest for the best tree by following a grid pattern, walking in straight lines (well, as straight as you could go with moving around the trees), so the compasses really helped.

Together, they started off into the woods single file and walking slowly, inspecting the trees around them as they went.

In about 15 minutes they came in sight of the creek. So far, no luck. All the trees were small. So they paced off thirty steps to the right and started walking back towards the park, keeping an eye on the compass.

An hour later and several passes back and forth between the park and the creek, they were getting closer to the boys' tree, which was in the center of the woods. The girls stopped for a drink, a rest and a snack at the edge of the park.

"All the trees are *small*," complained Alice.

"Not a single one we could build a tree house in, anyway," sighed Susan.

"We'll start from the far side next," said Amanda. "We don't want to be near those boys."

Becky agreed. "There must be another big tree in there *somewhere*, right?"

Amanda was getting a little worried. The woods did not seem as big as they used to be, now that they were getting to know them better. "Time to get moving!" she said, as she stood up and adjusted her backpack.

The other girls zipped up their backpacks and got up. They walked over to the far side of the woods, closest to the school. They lined up again, reset their compasses and started their search pattern again.

There must be another big tree! hoped Amanda.

A little over an hour later, they girls stopped near the boys' tree.

The Tree Hunt

"Not a single tree we can use!" muttered Alice.

"Not a one", agreed Susan.

"We'll just have to give up!" groaned Becky.

"Let me think, let me think," said Amanda. "We *can't* let those boys win!"

Amanda paced around in a circle, looking at the trees around her, hoping another perfect tree would magically appear. She even closed her eyes a few times and quickly opened them again. No luck.

There was only *one tree* in the whole forest that you could build a tree house in. And the boys were in it!

Ben was going to win!

Amanda stopped pacing and turned to face the other girls. She opened her mouth to speak and suddenly stopped. She quickly turned around and looked again at the massive tree, just visible behind a row of smaller trees.

It's a free forest… she thought.

"It's a free forest!" she cried. "And it's a *huge* tree!" She turned back to the other girls, her face lit up. "It's a huge tree… *and the boys are only building on one side!*"

The other girls looked back at her like she had gone crazy.

"What do you mean?" asked Susan. "The boys got there first. It's their tree!"

"Really? It's not actually *their* tree – they are just using it. And they didn't even *ask*. And they are only using *part of it*. Dad said I could use the wood from our yard too – and I claim *half*. And if the boys only have half the wood – they can't build in the whole tree. It's so big they probably won't even be able to use a quarter of the tree, maybe even less!" Amanda smiled triumphantly.

Becky looked uncertain. "I'm not sure that will work. What if the boys say no?"

Alice added "They are *Boys*, of course they will say no!"

"So what are we going to do?" asked Susan.

"We are going to do the smart thing. We are going to tell the boys *they will have to share*, or we will ask our parents to make us all share. The last thing any of us kids wants is to have our parents sticking their noses into kids business. If the boys call our bluff, we can ask the parents, and we might win that way and the boys lose. Or maybe the boys will just see reason and let us use half the tree. Either way – we can get half a tree to build our tree house!" declared Amanda.

"And hopefully no parents!" smiled Susan.

"Great idea!" agreed Alice.

The Tree Hunt

Becky still looked uncertain but was starting to warm up to the idea.

The four girls marched over to the near side of the tree, opposite from where they boys were building and arguing as usual. The girls began to inspect the tree and the branches. It took a few minutes for the boys to notice the activity on the far side of the clearing. Tom was up in the tree house, but Tim, James and Ben walked over to where the girls were making notes.

"What are you doing here?" demanded Ben.

"Planning our tree house," declared Amanda, again stretching up to her full height.

"You can't build here! It's *our* tree!" insisted Ben, getting red in the face.

"No, it's not *your* tree…it's a free forest!" retorted Amanda. She then explained their terms – and why the boys should agree to share the tree and "avoid trouble".

"But that's….that's blackmail!" groaned James.

"No, it's not. It's just fair. Dad said I could have half the wood, and we could build a tree house too. This is the only tree in the whole forest – maybe even our part of town – that is big enough to have a good tree house and that isn't already in someone else's yard. There is no reason not to share. It's so big, you won't even be able to see our tree house from yours!" finished Amanda.

Ben considered this. He knew his parents were all about "being fair" and he also knew that if he didn't share and Amanda told on him, Dad might take away Ben's wood – and then there wouldn't be a tree house anyway.

"Okay then, deal. But we divide up the wood in our back yard – Boys' pile and Girls' pile - and you girls build as far away from us as possible," muttered Ben.

Tom had hopped down out of the tree to see what was going on. All four of the boys looked unhappy – but they didn't want to lose their wood supply, or worse, have their parents poking around. The boys turned to walk back to their side of the tree. At the halfway mark, Ben dragged a line in the dirt with the heel of his shoe in one direction, and then went around to the other side of the tree and did the same thing, dividing the clearing into two halves, with the tree in the middle of the line.

"You girls stay on your side of the tree and the clearing. You will have to go all the way around to get your wood in!" said Ben, with a smirk.

Then he turned and stalked off towards the boys' tree house.

"The girls will have farther to go, it will be harder for them," he muttered quietly to the other boys. "Besides, do you think they are really going to build a tree house? They will get tired just bringing over all that wood."

Ben spoke even more quietly so the other boys had to come closer. "If they bring all that wood over to the tree *and give up*...the wood will be ours, and we won't have to carry it all the way here!"

All four boys smiled at that thought. *It was a lot of work carrying the boards to the tree, why not let the girls do most of the hard work? They would give up soon enough!*

10. Do We Have Enough Wood?

The next day, the girls started separating the boards into four piles in the back yard, so the boys and the girls each had fence slats and fence rails. Ben was standing there supervising the division of the boards to make sure it was done fairly. He wasn't going to actually help *move* the boards – it was the girls' idea after all.

"How many boards do you boys have at the tree already?" asked Amanda.

Ben counted the boards in his head. He thought about exaggerating with a lower number but decided not to. They could count them pretty easily when they went to the tree. "Thirty fence slats and six long boards, but we didn't use any fence posts."

Do We Have Enough Wood?

"Aw, were they too heavy?" smirked Amanda.

Ben started to get red in the face. "No, of course not! We just decided we don't need them. You girls can have them – *if* you can lift them!"

The girls spent most of the time before dinner moving their boards into piles. When they were finished, the piles looked a lot smaller, except for the fence posts which did not need to move. It didn't look like nearly half the quantity of wood that they had started with – it looked like a lot less, now that it was spread out around the yard.

The girls' pile had:

- 60 fence slats

- 10 fence rails

The boys' pile had:

- 30 fence slats

- 4 fence rails

On one side were the stack of 9 fence posts of varying lengths – the bottoms had been concreted into the ground and had to be dug up. Their father had cut the fence posts off above the ground with a chainsaw and then dug up the bases and took the concreted parts to the dump on the trailer.

Susan looked concerned. "It looked like a lot when we started, but now it doesn't look like we have that much to build with. **Do you think we have enough wood**?"

Amanda replied, "We will make sure it is enough."

Ben looked over at the boys' pile, which had thirty-six boards less than the girls, because the others were already at the tree. *Looks pretty skimpy*, he thought. *Maybe we won't be able to make our tree house as big as we thought!*

Becky looked quizzically at Amanda. "How can we be sure it is enough?"

Amanda looked quickly over at Ben and shook her head and whispered, "Not here, *he* will overhear us. Let's go inside and wash up and we can talk."

Ben remained standing in the back yard, looking at the much smaller pile of wood left on the boys' side, wondering what he was going to say to the other boys. He shook his head and counted them again. *One, two, three…*

The four girls went inside and washed up, then gathered in the kitchen to have a glass of milk. "Ok, how can you be sure we will have enough wood?" asked Becky.

Amanda started to speak but Alice interrupted. "We will have enough

wood…because…because we will *plan with it*!"
she stated. "We can count and measure the
wood, and then see how it will fit in the tree.
We can measure the branches and stuff, and
see what we can do with the wood we have!"

Susan mulled that over. "Your Dad said we
needed to *plan*, and figure out stuff before we
started to build. Let's look over our plan and
see how our ideas will work with the wood we
have."

Amanda's mother came into the kitchen and
started to set the dinner table. "Can you please
help me set the table, dear? I think it's time for
your friends to head home for their dinner too."

"Yes, Mom."

"We can start that tomorrow," whispered
Amanda as she turned back to her friends.
"Let's each figure out what else we have at
home – rope, nails, tools and other stuff that
our parents will let us use. Make a list of
everything and we can meet back here
tomorrow morning. Oh – and bring a
measuring tape and a level!"

The boys arrived early the next morning at
Ben's house, where he showed the other boys
how few boards were left in their pile. They
stared at the remaining boards, shoulders
slumped.

The Ultimate Tree House *Project!*

"We haven't even started on the Comic room," sighed Ben.

"Or the Watch tower," said Tom.

"Or the bowling alley," grunted James as he surveyed the yard, looking enviously at the girls' comparatively large pile of wood. "It doesn't seem fair!"

"I double-counted, they have half, like Dad said we had to split it," said Ben.

"We could still make the trap door and a few other things," suggested Tim.

"Got any hinges?" challenged Ben.

"Um no, we don't…" started Tim.

"Then we can't have a trap door!" interrupted Ben in frustration. "So much for our *Ultimate Tree House*, and it's all those stupid girls' fault!"

The other three boys muttered in agreement.

"We will just have to improvise, and finish first. We can still beat the girls!" exclaimed James. "If we work really hard they won't ever catch up!"

The other boys considered this.

"Let's grab some more boards and get moving!" commanded Ben.

Do We Have Enough Wood?

The boys divided into pairs and picked up several boards, then started walking towards the park with renewed energy.

We can still win! thought James.

The boys had been working for nearly an hour when the girls showed up at the tree with their backpacks , carrying one railing board and one fence slat between them. *They didn't even bring a full load of wood!* thought James. *They will take forever to get started if they think that much wood was heavy!*

The other boys turned to watch the girls and laughed. "You can't build a tree house if you don't bring any wood!" called out Tom.

"You'll see!" snapped back Susan.

The girls walked around the edge of the clearing over to "their" side of the tree and got to work. Where the girls were huddled it was very hard for the boys to see what they were doing, without actually going around the edge of the tree. *That was good – because maybe they wouldn't be bothered by the girls or have to look at them. On the other hand, what were they doing over there?* thought Ben. He couldn't get to a spot where he could see the girls without making it obvious that he was spying on them.

They only got occasional glimpses of the girls as they walked around, stretching something out and then huddling in a circle again.

What were they up to??

On the other side of the tree, the girls were doing lots of measuring, drawing and making notes. Becky had the tape measure and was recording measurements. Susan was holding up the fence slat between the branches to see which had closer spacing, and which branches were the most level if you put a board across them. Amanda put the level on top of the slat and took notes on a little pad.

Alice was sitting on the ground, looking up at the tree and making sketches of the branches, writing down numbers as Becky called them out to her. She was also making notes on each of the branches she drew as Susan and Amanda moved around the tree, testing the gaps between the branches. At every new branch, Amanda would jump up high and hang off of it to see how much it moved. She periodically brought Alice her note pad, who then read Amanda's notes and made some corrections and further notes on the drawing.

Do We Have Enough Wood?

Sounds of bickering and the occasional "Ow!"
came through from the boys' side of the tree
as the girls worked.

Alice had several pages of drawings and notes
by the time Amanda called the girls back
together. "I think that's pretty good for now,"
she said, "we can finish up after we have lunch
at my house."

The boys were still working hard on their tree
house when the girls walked back around the
edge of the clearing. "Where are you taking
those boards?" asked Tim, who had worked up
a sweat. The girls were carrying the fence slat
and railing board back to the house with them.
"Don't you trust us? You can't take your tree
house home with you, you know!"

"Besides, we don't want them, those boards
have *girl germs*!" said Ben.

The girls stuck out their tongues and kept
walking. "It's a *seeecret*!" taunted Susan over
her shoulder before they disappeared into the
smaller trees.

Tim stood at the edge of the clearing, looking
at the far side of the tree. *What were those
girls up to? It didn't look like they were building
anything!*

After lunch, the girls pulled out their planning

papers and Alice's drawings from the tree. Amanda had already counted the number of boards and how long each type of board was before the girls arrived in the morning, so they wouldn't waste any time.

Amanda asked her father, who was watching TV in the living room, if she could borrow the calculator from his office. "Sure, honey, just put it back when you are done. How is the tree house coming?"

"Just great, Dad," replied Amanda.

At that moment, Ben came into the kitchen to eat the sandwich his mother had left out for him. It was already starting to dry out at the edges. "*Tree house?*" snorted Ben. "They aren't building *anything*. They actually brought their wood *back to our house!*"

The other girls had quietly moved together to block Ben's view of the pile of notes on the kitchen table.

Amanda's father looked at her with a raised eyebrow. "Is that right, dear?"

"That's right Dad," she said, "just like we *planned.*"

Her father gave her a little smile. "Very good dear, I am sure it will be a great tree house."

Ben looked at his father, turned to Amanda and then back to his father. "You two are nuts," he snorted, "us boys are actually *building* a tree house, and it is going to be *awesome*. You *girls* aren't doing *anything*!" At that, he took a quick gulp of water, grabbed the rest of his sandwich, and started walking to the front door. "No time to stand around like you *girls*, we *boys* have a tree house to build!"

As the front door closed, Amanda winked at her father and turned back to the girls. "So do we! Now let's get to work!"

After Ben left, the girls quickly spread out the drawings across the top of the table. They put the list of equipment and materials on the left side, and spread out their planning documents in the middle. Amanda had a small pile of blank paper to make notes.

"Great drawings, Alice!" praised Amanda. "It looks like we have enough information to start doing some good planning."

She pointed at the materials list. "We have 10 fence rails, 60 fence slats – and 9 fence posts if we can use them. How does that look for fitting the branches, Susan?"

Susan leaned over the table and pointed at one of the drawings. "Well, not many pairs of branches are level to each other, and the ones that are look like they are wider apart than the fence slats in some places. So we will have to use the fence rails to start on the floor. Then we can put the fence slats across the fence rails and nail them down – about 12 of them, I think. But we might want to put a fence rail in the middle, because those fence slats look pretty thin – so probably 3 fence rails. "

Amanda thought about it for a moment. "Great idea, Susan. Better to use an extra board than risk an accident. Okay Becky, how about the measurements for the rope ladder?"

Becky pointed to another drawing. "If we space the rungs apart the same height as the steps in a house, it shouldn't be too hard for getting up into the tree. We should really tie the ropes up to the next higher branch, so I think we will need about 8 boards for rungs. The fence slats are pretty thin, so we will need to use a fence rail. If we cut one fence rail up into 6 pieces and a couple sections out of another one, that should be just about right for climbing if we drill holes for the rope. We don't want the rope ladder to be too heavy."

Amanda smiled. "Great work! So let's see what we have used up so far." She began to write on a blank piece of paper:

Used:

- 4 1/3 fence rails

- 12 fence slats

Do We Have Enough Wood?

Remainder:

- 5 2/3 fence rails

- 48 fence slats

- 9 fence posts

Amanda put down the pencil. "Hmm… we will run out of fence railings pretty quickly. But we have enough to do more than one level anyway – and we may be able to use the fence posts. What do you think, Alice?"

Alice inspected the drawings and rubbed her chin. "I think that's good – it gives us a good lower platform that will fit all of us. But I think we should make it harder for the boys to get up. We need to be able to pull up the rope ladder, especially when we are not in it. My Dad took down the old clothes line that ran from our top deck to the fence, but he kept the two pulleys and the wire. I will ask him if we can use them," she pointed to one of the branches in the middle sketch. "We can probably tie one up here, just above the rope ladder, and then we can tie off the wire when we don't need it. And then…" she trailed off, thoughtful.

"What?" asked Amanda.

"Well, I was thinking we have two pulleys. We only need one for the rope ladder, and not all of the time. So maybe we could setup two pulleys, to help us lift stuff up onto the platform?" Alice looked around at the other girls to see what they thought of the idea.

"Brilliant!" smiled Becky, "that will definitely make it easier. Amanda's Dad was so smart telling us to take time to plan. This will make it so much easier and faster to build our tree house!"

"We could make two hooks and put them on the end of each wire. Then we could tie stuff together and hook through the ropes at each end," added Amanda.

"This planning stuff is great!" agreed Susan.

"You know what?" said Amanda, "This calls for a celebration. Mom, can we have a cookie?" she called out into the living room.

"Sure, honey – one each, and cleanup after," her Mother called back.

Amanda opened the cookie jar and the girls each selected a cookie. Amanda poured some more milk into their glasses. She put the milk away and then raised her glass. "To success!" she said.

The other three girls raised their glasses. "To our tree house!" they chorused.

In the living room, Amanda's father quietly smiled behind his newspaper.

Do We Have Enough Wood?

11. The Accident

The following Saturday, the boys spent as much time as they could at the tree, working on the tree house, bringing over a few boards at a time and banging and sawing away. However, they still did not have a rope ladder. Although they were no longer worried about the girls getting into their tree house, they had still not figured out how to make a proper rope ladder. They had made a few attempts but the rope always kept slipping. James had tied the rope over the branch and Tom had started to climb it. He got half way up when the rope suddenly came loose and Tom fell hard onto a protruding section of the tree root. He was still able to work on the tree house, but he now had a big shiny bruise on the top of his leg.

The Accident

That afternoon, the girls showed up at the tree with coils of rope looped over their shoulders, and some very short boards. They walked around to the girls' side of the tree, and Alice quietly climbed onto Becky's shoulders and scrambled up onto a low branch. She took off the first rope and uncoiled it, and then tied it securely to the branch above her. She moved over a bit and tied the second rope onto the branch, about a short board width apart from the first one.

Amanda then picked up the first short board from the pile on the ground, and threaded the first rope through one of the holes they had drilled at her house with her father's drill. She repeated this with the second rope, sliding it through the hole on the other end of the board.

She slid the board up as high as she could reach, and then Alice tied a simple knot in the rope and snugged it tight. Alice lifted up the other end of the board while Amanda watched. "A little bit higher," she called out. Alice slid the board up a bit higher and then tied a knot. The top rung of the ladder was reasonably level. Susan jumped up and grabbed onto the wood, testing that the knots were secure. The ropes and the board held firm.

Becky helped Susan thread the next board onto the ropes, while Amanda stood back and judged the height and level. Alice tied the knots for the second board like she had for the first, because it was still a little high for Susan and Becky to reach. Becky and Susan threaded the remaining boards onto the ropes and tied the knots for each in turn, until the last board was just above ground level. It had only taken about twenty minutes to assemble the rope ladder.

"Great job!" called out Amanda. "Becky, please take the *secret package* up to Alice and help her set it up."

Becky slipped her backpack back on and quickly climbed the rope ladder while Susan steadied it. Alice helped her swing over to the branch she was sitting on. Alice stayed by the rope ladder while Becky moved over two arms-lengths from Alice. She then opened her backpack and pulled out two pulleys and two short lengths of rope. She handed one pulley and one length of rope to Alice, and together they tied the pulleys securely onto the higher branch, adding a couple extra half-hitches just to be safe. Becky unzipped her backpack again and pulled out two coils of plastic-coated wire. Each one had a blunt metal hook fastened onto the end. She passed one coil to Alice. They each found the thin end of their wire and threaded it through the top of the pulley, facing away from them. They lowered the thin end of the wires down to the ground, keeping the hook end hanging just below their feet where Susan could reach them.

"All set?" asked Amanda.

The Accident

"Yep!" replied Alice.

"All secure!" said Becky.

Susan pulled on the ropes hanging down from the pulleys. "Ready!" called Susan.

First Alice and then Becky climbed down the rope ladder. Susan pulled on the two hooks and put them around the ropes under the middle board, and then pulled gently on the free ends of the wires so that they were snug. The rope ladder started to lift up. She carefully pulled on the two wires until the rope ladder was nearly over her head.

She then carefully looped the wires together and tied the loop over the end of another small branch, as high as she could reach.

"All set!" declared Susan.

"Time for a break!" said Amanda, and the four girls started to walk back to the house. After the girls disappeared into the trees, the four boys walked around the edge of the trunk to take a look at what the girls were up to. From where they stood, they couldn't see anything very clearly – the rope ladder was just out of sight.

What were those girls up to?

Back at the house, the girls had a quick drink of water and then Amanda pulled out a pencil, and a piece of paper folded neatly into quarters.

"Rope ladder: check!" she marked it off the schedule.

"Secret package: check!" she marked off the pulleys on the list.

"OK, next is the first 3 railing boards and the 10 fence slats. Stage 2 is the railing boards. Stage 3 is the fence slats. Now – tools. Becky and Alice, you have the hammers?" asked Amanda.

"Check!" replied Becky.

"Yes!" called out Alice.

"Susan – nails?"

"Check!" said Susan.

"Rope?"

"Check!" Alice smiled.

"And I have the measuring tape for later," said Amanda. "Ok, we're ready to go!"

The girls divided up the railing boards, two to the taller pair and one board to the smaller pair of girls. They walked over through the park, through the trees and they arrived at the tree to hear the boys arguing – again.

The Accident

The girls skirted the clearing and went around to their side of the tree. While Susan reached up and untied the wires and lowered the rope ladder, Becky, Amanda and Alice placed the three boards down facing the branch head-on. When the rope ladder was free from the wire hooks, Alice climbed up the ladder. Susan, Amanda and Becky lifted the first board up and pointed it up over the branch, beside Alice. They lifted it up and began to slide it up and over the edge of the branch, while Alice guided it into position. They then repeated the process for the next two boards. When the boards were in place and roughly parallel, Becky climbed the ladder and together then began to nail the three boards down to the branch they were sitting on. Then they carefully walked on the boards to the other branch, holding onto the branches above. They sat down on the other branch and then secured each board with two nails.

"Done!" called out Becky.

The two girls climbed back down the rope ladder and Susan secured it back up into the tree, hooking the coil of wire onto the small branch.

The girls walked back to the house, and ten minutes later they were back at the tree, with each pair of girls carrying 6 fence slats – plus one extra.

Susan repeated the retrieval of the rope ladder, while the others tied up the bundle of 13 boards with a rope at each end. When the ropes were securely tied around the bundles of wood, Alice and Becky climbed the rope ladder while Susan and Amanda slipped the blunt hooks between the knots and the boards. Then they each took one wire and pulled on the free ends, lifting the boards up to where Becky and Alice waited. When the boards were above the level of the lower branches, Alice and Becky grabbed the bundle of boards and pulled them over onto the waiting fence rails. They unhooked the wires and began to untie the ropes.

Together, they spread twelve of the boards evenly across the length of the fence rails. Susan and Amanda climbed the rope ladder in turn and stood on the platform. Susan opened her backpack and pulled out the bag of nails, which she and Amanda handed to Alice and Becky one by one as they nailed twelve of the fence slats into the fence rails. Fairly quickly, the platform was completed, with Amanda and Susan helping to hold the fence slats in place so there were only small gaps. When they were finished, the resulting platform was the size of a full fence panel.

The four girls stood in the middle of the platform and smiled broadly and began to giggle. Becky looked like she was about to shout for joy when Susan stopped her. "Shhh!

We don't want the boys to know how we are doing!" she whispered.

"On to Stage four!" said Amanda. She pulled out the measuring tape from her backpack. Once again, Alice sat down to draw – this time, on the middle of the platform, high up in the tree. Becky and Amanda started measuring while Susan began testing the next level of branches by pulling down on them.

On the far side of the tree, the boys were starting to work on their second level. They had fence slats and railing boards spread out haphazardly across a number of branches, which formed a kind of maze. In some places they only had one or two boards nailed side by side, with the ends of the boards just reaching both branches. The boys had put in extra nails at the ends to make sure the boards were secure.

Tom, James and Ben were up in the tree, while Tim was on the ground, passing up boards one by one. Tim could hear the girls start calling out numbers to each other, but it was more muffled than before.

"They're counting again," said Tim.

"What?" hollered Ben.

"I said, the girls are counting again," replied Tim.

"Well, go see what they are doing this time – if they are actually doing *anything*," snorted Ben.

Tim walked around the trunk so that he could see the girls' side. The girls were nowhere to be seen – but Tim could hear them clearly. The only thing he could see – was a *rope ladder*.

Tim quickly walked back over to their tree house and whispered up at Ben. "I think they are up in the tree!"

"Well, go over and check then," grunted Ben, "Go and see what they are up to."

Tim walked to the edge of the line in the dirt that divided the boys' side from the girls' side. Feeling a bit nervous like he might get zapped by lightning or something, Tim gingerly stepped over the line and put his foot down on the ground.

No lightning, he thought, *or at least not today*.

As quietly as he could, he walked over to the rope ladder and looked up. What he saw there made his jaw drop. He ran back to the boys' side and shouted up at Ben. "They are up in the tree and they have a rope ladder and they have a tree house and it looks really good and strong!" he gushed, out of breath.

"WHAT!?!?!" shouted Ben, "No! It can't be! They can't! They are just stupid girls!! How did they sneak that by us?"

The Accident

Ben was jumping up and down on one of the thinner sections of the tree house as he shouted, stamping his feet. He was standing where the branches were spread far apart and there were only a few boards. He stamped in the middle of two fence slats when they suddenly snapped. "Whaaaaa!" yelled Ben, as he started to fall. He caught his foot on the edge of the broken board, flipped over backwards and fell to the ground. He landed awkwardly and Tim heard another loud snap. Tim looked up to see if another board had broken.

"**Waaaaaaaaaaaiiiiiiiiieeeeeeeeee!**" screamed Ben and then fainted.

Tim spun around to where Ben lay sprawled on the ground, his left leg twisted at a funny angle.

"**Help! Help! Help!**" yelled Tim at the top of his lungs. James and Tom quickly jumped down out of the tree and hurried over to where Ben lay, unmoving. The girls quickly climbed down out of the tree, ignoring the line scratched in the dirt as they ran over to the boys.

"What happened? What…" started Amanda and then she saw her brother. "WHAT HAPPENED?"

"Ben fell!" wailed Tim. "He was so mad you girls suddenly had a cool tree house from out of nowhere he was yelling and jumping up and down and then the boards broke and he flipped and fell and…" panted Tim. "Is he dead?"

Alice knelt down to touch Ben. His skin had turned pale but his chest was moving up and down. "He's not dead. But we need help quickly. Becky – you run back with Susan to Amanda's house and get her Mom or Dad. Amanda and I will stay with the boys and help Ben."

Amanda was looking shaken. "…*Ben?*" she whispered as she knelt down beside him.

Ben groaned faintly but did not stir.

Alice started looking over Ben without moving him. *There was no bleeding – which was good*, she thought. They had not done their first aid badge yet, but it would have been helpful. He was still pale but his breathing seemed normal, maybe a bit fast. She wasn't sure what that meant but she hoped he was ok.

Tim, Tom and James just looked on in horror.

"Is there anything we can do?" asked James.

Alice shook her head, tears in her eyes. "I don't know. *I don't know what else to do!*" she cried.

A couple minutes later, Becky and Susan came running into the clearing with Amanda's father.

The Accident

He glanced quickly up at the tree and then down at Ben and the seven children surrounding him.

He knelt down beside Ben and began to inspect him, gently feeling for any injuries other than the apparently broken leg. He gently touched Ben's face. "Hey sport, can you hear me?"

Ben moaned.

"We are going to have to move you, but carefully," said his father. He looked around the tree and spotted a few fence slats and a saw lying on the ground. "James – go grab a fence slat. Tom – Tim- one of you, go grab the saw."

The children panicked. "Don't cut off his leg!" wailed Amanda.

Her father shook his head. "No, I am not cutting off his leg. But I need something to splint his leg so it doesn't move much until we get him to the hospital. We need to get him there soon as it looks like he is in shock. Do any of you kids have some rope?" he looked around at the children.

"We do," said Becky. She took off her backpack and unzipped it. She pulled out two short segments of rope and handed them to Amanda's father.

"Great, that will be perfect. Boys – I want you to cut that fence slat to be about this long." He held his hands apart, roughly the length of Ben's lower leg. Tim and Tom steadied the board on a tree root while James started to saw the board. They brought over the cut board when they had finished.

"Ok, now I need you children to help me. We need a couple of you to roll Ben over just a bit, and hold him there so I can see his whole leg. Then I am going to very carefully lift his leg while one of you slides the board under it. Then quickly but gently, poke the two ropes under the board." He looked up at the children. Alice, James and Becky knelt down behind Ben. Tim and Tom each took a piece of rope and got ready. Amanda held the shortened board in her hands.

"Ok, ready? Slowly – slowly roll Ben towards you," he pointed "grab him there, there, and there." Alice, Becky and James carefully pulled on Ben's shoulder, arm and good leg and slowly rolled Ben towards them.

"Good, now stop and hold him there. I am going to lift his leg – very carefully." Her father gently lifted both ends of Ben's leg around the break. Ben moaned and mumbled something. "Amanda, you ready?" he looked over his shoulder at his daughter. She looked nervous.

"Yes, Dad," she said.

The Accident

"OK, now gently slide the board right under his leg," he directed. Amanda slid the fence slat into place. Her father then gently lowered Ben's leg onto the board, then lifted the board up just enough for the ropes to go underneath.

"Now, poke the ends of the ropes under the board." The two boys did so. "Now pull the ropes through about half way."

The boys pulled the ropes through as instructed.

Ben's father lowered the board onto the two ropes, took off his jacket and folded it over a few times. He gently lay it over Ben's leg, taking care to not touch the break. Next, he tied the ropes over the jacket, snug but firm, immobilizing the leg. Ben groaned and his eyelids fluttered. He still looked pale.

With the leg secured, Ben's father spoke to the children. "OK, he should be stable enough for me to lift him up and carry him to my car. But I am going to need some help getting him back through the trees without the branches hitting his leg. Can you kids pull back the branches as I carry Ben?"

The children all nodded.

Ben's father gently slipped his left hand under Ben's legs and his right hand under Ben's shoulders. He slowly stood up. "You are getting heavy, young man," he said. Ben mumbled something but his eyes remained closed.

The children walked ahead, looking for branches that were in the way and pulling them aside until Ben's father passed, then ran on ahead to get the branches up ahead. They soon emerged into the park, where Ben's father began to walk a little more quickly. The children followed close behind. They walked up to Ben's house and into the driveway.

"Amanda, get the car keys from my left pocket and open the back doors." She got out his keys and clicked the remote to unlock the car, then opened the back door nearest Ben. "Now go to the other side, open the door and get in. I need some help sliding Ben onto the back seat without bumping him too much."

Amanda went around the car and opened the door. She sat in the far seat and reached towards her Dad. He passed Ben into the car head first and Amanda helped slide Ben towards her, lifting his head and shoulders across as he was laid across the seat. Her father adjusted Ben to be more comfortable and closed the door. Ben's head was resting on Amanda's lap. She cautiously stroked his hair. Her father came around and closed her door. "Buckle up, honey," he said. She pulled the strap down across her lap and shoulders and clicked the seatbelt.

The Accident

The other children were gathered around the side of the car, looking very worried. Ben's father opened the driver side door and looked at the children before he got in. "Ben is going to be OK. It looks like he just has a broken leg, but we need to get him to the hospital so they can set it and check him over," he paused. "I am very proud of the way you children helped today. But we are going to have a talk about this tree house with your parents when we get back home from the hospital."

The children's faces fell and they suddenly looked more nervous than worried. *He was going to talk to their parents…!* In the back seat, Amanda's heart sunk into her stomach. *So much for our tree house building*, she thought, *and we just got started on the project.* Then she looked down at Ben lying across the seat, head in her lap and suddenly felt selfish and guilty. *Ben wouldn't have broken his leg if it wasn't for me wanting to build that tree house!*

Her father started the car and backed out of the driveway. They turned out onto the main street and drove off towards the hospital.

The remaining children watched the car disappear around the corner and then looked at the ground. They all hoped Ben would be ok. Alice gave Susan a short hug. Becky stepped forward and quickly hugged James and whispered "you were so brave!" and then stepped back. Tim and Tom looked back towards the forest and said together "We still have to get the tools and bring them back here."

The children slowly walked over towards the park together.

The Accident

12. Safety Inspection

The next day Ben came home from the hospital. He needed help getting out of the car, after he twisted sideways on the seat. His left leg was in a big white cast from his toes and stopped just above his knee. Amanda came around the car, holding a pair of crutches. Her mother helped lift Ben out of the car and steadied him on the crutches.

They started towards the front door when Susan, Alice, Tim and Tom spotted them and came over. Nobody was working on the tree house today – it kind of felt like there was maybe a curse on it now or something.

"You OK Ben?" asked Tim.

"OK I guess. The cast is really heavy. And they say I have to have it on for *six weeks*, and I am home from school for at least three weeks."

Safety Inspection

"That's not so bad, you can watch TV and play video games and stuff," offered Tom.

"Yes, though Mom says I still have to do school work at home," Ben looked at them sadly. "But...but...the worst thing is that Dad said I can't go up into any trees for at least two weeks after the cast is off!"

Tim and Tom looked at each other. *Two whole months of no tree house!*

"Poor Ben," said Susan.

Ben tried to glare at her but he was too tired and his leg hurt. The best he managed was a small grimace.

"Ben needs to go in and rest," said his mother. "You go on and play now, you can come back tomorrow after school and visit him."

"OK Mrs. Jones," said Alice.

Ben's father looked sternly at the children. "I phoned your parents this morning. We agreed that none of you are allowed near the tree until we do a safety check."

"But, but..." started Tom.

Ben's father shook his head. "This is non-negotiable. We don't want any more broken bones – or worse," he stated firmly.

The children hung their heads sadly as they walked towards the park.

The Ultimate Tree House *Project!*

The rest of the week the children stayed clear of the forest on the way to and from school, but peered deeply into the trees as they walked by, to try and catch a glimpse of the big tree. The forest was beginning to look darker and more menacing as each day passed.

On Saturday morning, all of the children gathered at Ben's house with their parents. Some of the parents carried tools – hammers and pry-bars. They kind of looked like a mob for hunting monsters – all they needed were some pitchforks. The children shifted uncomfortably from foot to foot while they waited for Ben's father to come out. *Maybe the tree really was a monster – it did break Ben's leg*, Tim thought.

Ben's Dad emerged from the garage with a leather tool belt strapped around his waist, with a few tools poking out here and there. "OK, let's go have a look and make sure this tree will be safe for our kids."

The group walked across the street and over into the park, the children straggling behind. Suddenly they felt afraid – but were they afraid of the tree – or afraid of what their parents might do?

"I don't wanna go in there," whispered James.

Safety Inspection

Becky softly took his hand and squeezed it. "Let's go in together," she said. She started to let go of his hand but he squeezed her hand too. *Maybe he is really afraid*, she thought. *It **was** really scary when Ben broke his leg.*

Tim and Tom walked behind the pair as Becky led James into the trees. James seemed to have a bit more confidence now.

The big tree became visible, towering above the other trees. The dark imaginings of the children disappeared as they entered the sun-dappled clearing. It didn't look scary at all.

The parents split up and several began inspecting the tree and the tree house on the boys' side. A couple of parents walked over to check the girls' tree house. The girls followed, but stood back from the adults. Becky's Dad inspected the platform and looked at the rope ladder suspended in the lower branches. He put his hands up over the edge of the platform and hung there with his full weight. He stood back up and walked over to the girls. "You girls built this?" he asked, raising an eyebrow.

Susan stepped forward. "Yes, sir, we did."

"Nothing wrong with this one. You are doing a fine job so far and the branches look strong," he smiled. "All clear from me."

They all walked over to the boys' side, where Tim, Tom and James stood on the side with trembling lips, fighting back tears with every bang of a hammer. There was an ever-growing pile of boards accumulating on the ground under the remnants of their tree house.

"These ones here, there is not enough support – the branches are too far apart again," pointed Amanda's father. Squeals from the nails as a pry bar lifted the board from the branches on each side. James' mother and father pulled down the boards from the tree. They hammered the nails back through the ends of the boards, pulled out the bent nails and threw the boards onto the pile. The nails went into a smaller pile by their feet. They would pick them up later.

An hour later, the boys' tree house was only a few scattered sections of boards across close branches – with large gaps in between the sections of the once-grand tree house. More than half of the wood that had been their *Ultimate Tree House* was lying in a pile on the ground next to the large mound of bent and useless nails.

"All done. The rest of the sections are OK," said Amanda's father. He turned to look at the three boys. "You need to have more support in your tree house, or you will have more accidents like Ben's." His face darkened. "That's why we pulled those other boards out. They were all too dangerous. We will leave the pile here so you can start again, but this time you have to have the boards put across closer branches, or use the longer boards for cross-bracing first."

James couldn't take it anymore. "What's the point?" he shouted, tears streaming down his face as he ran through the trees and headed for home.

Tim and Tom looked at the large pile of wood and at each other. Their shoulders slumped. It suddenly looked like a huge effort to rebuild – especially without Ben to help.

The other parents picked up their tools while James' parents picked up the mound of bent nails. His father inspected the last few bright, shiny nails thoughtfully before putting them into his pocket. They departed from the clearing, followed by the other parents and their children, until only Amanda and her father were left. "Let's go have a look at your tree house."

Amanda was suddenly nervous. *Becky's father said it was ok – but would my Dad?* She suspiciously eyed the hammer that he still held in his hand.

They walked over the boy-girl line, which had almost disappeared on one side amidst the shuffle of footprints. Her father walked around under the tree house, poking here, pulling there, and lightly tapping in a few places with his hammer. Every time he lifted the hammer towards the platform, her heart jumped.

126

"Hmmm, not bad, not bad at all," he mused. "I bet that would support a couple of adults at least, maybe three. Though I think you need to replace those metal hooks on the pulleys with something else." He turned to Amanda. "So how did you make such a better start to your tree house, do you think?"

She looked at the tree house and then back at her father. She wasn't sure but this felt like some type of a test. "Um, we measured the space between the branches and measured the boards and then counted them up at home and…" she paused. "Well, Dad, I guess we just did what you said to do. We thought about what we wanted and then figured out what we could do with what we had, and then we started to design it. And then we put it together."

Her father smiled broadly. "So, you *planned and then built*. Well done." He turned to point at the far side of the tree, where the boys' large pile of boards was clearly visible on the ground. "Do you see what can happen when you don't plan?"

Amanda looked over at the boys side and suddenly felt sad for them. "You have to start again?" she said softly.

"Not only that – but people can get hurt – like your brother did. In my business, if people don't plan and they make mistakes, people can

– and sometimes do – get badly injured or even killed."

Amanda remembered something from the newspaper last year. Her father had been quite upset because someone he knew had been badly hurt when the wall of a new building collapsed because someone had made a mistake.

"Well, what is done is done. Ben was lucky it was just a broken leg, and the boys' side is safe, for now. What you girls are doing is just fine – keep planning and building, but always remember to make sure you have good supports like this platform," he smacked the edge of the platform with the flat of his hand. "Who knows, you might become a builder someday, like your Dad!"

Together, they turned and walked towards home.

13. Girls in the House

Several days later, James was still upset and had not come back to work on the tree. At school the previous day, Becky had approached James at recess to ask if he was OK. James said "Yah, sure," and had looked down at the ground, rolling small bits of gravel around with the tip of his left shoe.

"Don't you want to finish the tree house?" Becky asked softly.

James snorted. "It's not a tree house, it's a *wreck*. I don't know why we bothered."

"But you can start again...?" she offered.

James waved his hands in the air. "It was a *masterpiece*. And now all of our parents *ruined* it. We wouldn't know where to begin. So why bother?" He turned and walked away from Becky, shaking his head.

By the following Friday, the girls had made steady progress on their tree house, measuring and drawing and taking notes, then coming back with enough boards to add the next part. By now they had three platforms, the second two slightly smaller than the first, built between higher branches on either side.

The girls were trying to figure out if they should add wooden ladders between the sections and how they would add railings on the platforms when they heard two of the boys talking on the far side of the tree. Tim and Tom had come back to work on the tree house each day after the inspection, but they were not making much progress with just the two of them working on it. There was still a substantial pile of boards lying on the ground beside the tree.

Ben was stuck at home while his leg started to mend, and Amanda was bringing home schoolwork for him each day. He said he would be be able to go back to school (on crutches) in another week or so, but he would have to take it easy. That also meant that he would not be allowed near the tree for a long time, in case he jarred his leg or tripped on a tree root. The doctor had been very, very clear about that part when they were still in the hospital, and his mother had nodded firmly. "No going to the tree house until summer."

Ben had stuck out his jaw and said "Awww Mom!" but she shook her head. "Sorry Ben, it's too risky. The doctor said if you re-break your leg, it will end up shorter and you would end up walking lop-sided." Ben had just sighed and closed his eyes.

The girls were finishing up for the afternoon; it was almost dinner time. They walked past Tim and Tom as they headed towards the park. They walked straight through the clearing, instead of around it. During the "inspection", the dirt line indicating "boys' side/girls' side" was almost completely erased by a mass of big and small footprints. Nobody had bothered to re-draw the line.

"How's it going, Tom?" asked Susan as she peered up into the remainder of the boys' tree house. Since the accident – and the *inspection*, the girls all felt a bit sorry for the boys.

Tom grunted. "Slow. It is really hard to find branches that are close enough together on this side of the tree." He picked up a fence slat and propped it on top of two branches. The ends barely went past the branches – sitting there, it looked just like the one that broke Ben's leg. He shrugged and pulled the board back. "See what I mean?"

"I'm sure you will find some good branches," offered Alice, but she looked doubtful. When you examined the tree closely, the branches really were further apart on this side of the tree. Maybe it had something to do with the direction it faced, and the sun or something. She wasn't sure.

"You boys going home for dinner?" asked Amanda.

"Almost done," said Tim. "One more nail." He banged on a nail with the hammer, occasionally missing it. He didn't seem to have his heart in it.

"See you at school then," called Becky. She pulled her collar around her neck as the girls walked off through the trees. It was starting to get a bit windy. As they emerged into the grassy field of the park, Amanda looked back towards the big tree, now hidden by the rows of smaller trees. She, too pulled up her collar around her neck. A strong gust of wind blew her hair forward around her face. She brushed it back and looked at the tops of the trees, which were starting to bend in the wind, like they were slowly waving goodbye. The girls walked quickly through the park and across the street, pulling their jackets close around them.

When Amanda arrived home, her mother opened the door and looked out across the park at the moving tree tops. "The weatherman says a big storm is coming this weekend.

Feels like it is not too far away. Come on inside, dinner is ready."

Amanda walked in past her mother and took off her jacket. She shivered, then slipped off her boots and headed upstairs to wash up for dinner.

Outside, a low moan began to rise as the wind blew harder against the house.

14. The Storm

"It's a big one, all right," said Amanda's father on Saturday morning. Outside, it was still quite dark even though it was past 10 o'clock. The wind made a steady howl as it tugged against the edge of the window frames. "We'll be fine in the house. However, we should get out the candles and flashlights in case we lose power tonight." Amanda went to the closet in the hallway where they kept the emergency stuff, pulled out two plastic containers and put them on the kitchen table.

The weather forecaster on the TV was saying it was a big low pressure system that had come inland from the far away coast. It had been a hurricane until two days ago, but it had slowed down and weakened when it made landfall. They were saying it still had plenty of energy in it, and they were expecting high winds and lots of rain for their town and surrounding area. Amanda and her parents went out to bring in all the loose stuff from the yard and put it away in the garage, where the cars were already safely parked. They even brought in the glass-top patio table. "But it's heavy!" said Amanda, finding it hard to imagine *just wind* moving it as her parents carried it in through the garage side door.

"You'd be surpised what a strong wind can do," said her father. "If you get a strong enough wind, it can lift a house."

Amanda looked up at their house, two stories high and covered with wood siding. It looked strong, and it was hard to imagine it blowing away. *Like the Wizard of Oz*, she thought.

"Don't worry honey – it would take a really big wind to do anything to our house. But the loose stuff in the yard might move and hit something so we are putting it away just in case," smiled her father.

She helped her parents bring in the last few things from the yard, including some toys and a soccer ball. They closed the door and went inside to have some hot chocolate. Ben was sitting on the couch, watching cartoons and playing a video game on his mother's tablet. His left leg was propped up on a foot stool. "How are you doing, son?" asked Ben's father.

"Ungh," muttered Ben. The novelty of staying home and watching as much TV as he wanted was starting to wear off.

His father patted him on the head and asked "Want some hot chocolate, Ben?"

"Yes please, Dad."

A whistling sound came from the kitchen. The jug had boiled and Amanda and her mother were making the hot chocolate, adding some milk and a marshmallow to each cup. They brought their cups out into the living room to keep Ben company while they each sipped their cup of hot chocolate.

Ben wasn't paying attention to the TV. He was staring out the window, watching the wind lash the tops of the trees across the park. "Hope the tree house is ok," he muttered.

That night, Ben and Amanda had a hard time getting to sleep. The wind had picked up and was really howling outside, and they could hear the trees in the neighborhood banging against fences and houses. Occasionally they heard a loud crash, which made them jump. Ben finally drifted off into a troubled sleep, with dreams of trees chasing him down a forest path, branches waving and crashing into each other.

The Storm

Amanda awoke to the sun streaming through an opening in the curtain. She got out of bed, rubbed her eyes and pulled the curtain aside. She saw a lot of broken branches lying around their yard, and a few broken fences in neighboring yards. *Good thing we brought our stuff in*, she thought. *But at least nobody's house blew away!*

Her bedroom was on the back side of the house, so she had to go into the living room to get a view of the park. Ben was already in the kitchen eating breakfast. He had the crutches leaning against his chair.

Amanda walked up to the living room window and looked out over the park. There were a lot of broken branches strewn throughout the park, with a few trees completely uprooted near the edge. It looked like they had fallen into the forest.

The tree house! She panicked. "Mom, we need to go check the tree house and make sure it is ok!"

Her mother was sitting at the kitchen table, buttering some toast. "Not yet dear. Have some breakfast first – and you aren't even dressed." She put down her piece of toast and took a sip of coffee. "Besides, your father wants to do another inspection. Some trees blew over last night, and he wants to make sure that what you have built in the tree is still safe."

Inspection! Amanda grew worried. *What if the storm wrecked the tree or their tree house, and the parents ended up taking them all apart?* Suddenly she didn't feel hungry, but her mother was watching her so she sat down at the table and poured herself a bowl of cereal and began to eat it.

An hour later (though it felt like much, much longer), Amanda was putting on her boots to go inspect the tree with her father. She had asked if she could call the other kids to see if they could come, and now they were all assembled outside, waiting for Amanda and her father to emerge. James was with them. Together, they all walked through the park, stepping high over the smaller branches and walking around the larger ones.

The regular pathway that led to the tree was blocked by several small uprooted trees, so they had to walk around. After navigating through more broken branches, they finally came to the tree. Tim and Tom gasped together as they saw what had happened to the big tree.

The Storm

"Oh...No!!!"

A medium-sized tree had broken off just above the ground and fallen into the branches of the big tree. The big tree itself looked relatively undamaged, but the same could not be said for the boys' tree house. The fallen tree had smashed directly through the main platform.

"I was just nailing that the other day!" wailed Tim.

"It's all ruined, all of it!" cried Tom.

James didn't say anything. He just stared at the wreckage.

"OK kids, we will come back to this in a few minutes. Let's go check the girls' side," said Amanda's father.

Amanda was afraid to look. She squeezed her eyes shut as they walked around the trunk of the tree, looking down and opening them up just enough to avoid tripping on the tree roots.

"Well!" said her father.

Becky pulled on Amanda's elbow. "Look!"

"I don't want to!" whispered Amanda. "Is it OK?"

"See for yourself," said Alice.

Amanda opened her eyes and looked up.

Aside from a few small scattered branches lying on the ground underneath it, the girls' side of the tree was untouched. Her father had already walked over to the platform and was inspecting it. "No loose boards, and I don't see any cracked branches. It looks like you girls were lucky to build on this side."

"OK, let's go back and take a closer look at the other side," said Amanda's father. They slowly walked over to the boys' side. The pile of wood that had been removed the prior week was sitting clear of the fallen branches, but the rest of the tree house was a shambles. Apart from a few small sections, the tree had ripped out or smashed most of the boards. "We will have to pull down the broken boards and the hanging ones with nails sticking out to make them safe, but the rest I think we just have to leave. No telling when the council will get around to cutting up the fallen trees. There were a lot of trees blown down last night, and some fell on houses."

He looked at the faces of the children, who had formed a loose half-circle in front of him. "*Nobody* can build on this side of the tree right now, is that clear? It's just too dangerous."

The boys look stricken. "No more tree house..." started James.

"All that work!" said Tim.

"...all wasted," added Tom.

The Storm

"Who's gonna tell Ben?" asked James. He turned to look at Amanda.

She looked back at him. "I don't want to do it, he will just think I am lying and being mean."

Amanda's father put his hand on her shoulder and sighed. "I will tell Ben."

Alice looked thoughtful. "You know, it is lucky your tree house was pulled apart by our parents." Six children turned to look at her like she was crazy. "I mean, if our parents hadn't done that *safety inspection* then all the boards would have been busted up from the storm last night. This way, the boys still have most of their wood," she pointed at the pile of boards.

James looked at the pile of wood that was clear of the fallen tree, then he looked over at the girls' tree house. *Maybe...* he thought, *just maybe.*

As they walked back through the trees to the park, James tapped Tim and Tom on the shoulder. "I have an idea," he whispered. "Come over to my house after," he said to the twins. They both raised their eyebrows at exactly the same time. Weird. *What is he up to?* wondered Tim.

15. No More Nails!

Ben did not take the news very well at all. He insisted everyone was lying – even his father. What made it worse was that he could not go out into the forest to see the tree for himself. "You are all just mean, horrible people and *I hate you*!" He stumped off to his bedroom, crutch-foot-crutch-foot and then slammed the door. The sound of loud music blared from his room as he turned on his little stereo.

Amanda had pulled out the project plans and sketches and spread them around the kitchen table. There were still some things to figure out about adding the railings, and whether they needed wood or rope ladders between sections. She had a pencil held sideways between her lips, lost in thought, when the front doorbell rang.

No More Nails!

She went down the stairs and looked through the peep hole. Tim, Tom and James stood outside on the doorstep.

"Ben's in a bad mood, he thinks we are all lying about the tree," stated Amanda. "I don't think he wants any visitors right now."

James stepped forward. "Um...we don't want to talk to Ben right now. Actually, we would like...um...to talk...to *you*."

"And the other girls," added Tim.

"We have an idea," finished Tom.

Amanda raised an eyebrow. "Oh really? I guess you can come in, and I will call the other girls. Take off your shoes – Mom says everyone has to."

The four children walked up the stairs into the kitchen. Tim noticed the papers on the kitchen table and started walking towards them. "Unh-uh," said Amanda. "*Girl stuff*. You boys go sit in the living room. I will call Becky, Alice and Susan to see if they can come over."

The boys went and sat on the couch while Amanda went into the kitchen to make some phone calls.

Fifteen minutes later, all seven children were gathered in the living room. Ben was still

144

sulking down in his room, the music turned up loud.

"OK, so what is your idea – and what does it have to do with us?" asked Amanda, though she actually had a fair idea what they were going to ask.

James looked uncomfortable. "Um, well, you see..."

Amanda was starting to get impatient. "What?"

James let it all rush out. "We-want-to-build-a-tree-house-with-you-can-we-pleeeeease?"

The four girls looked suprised.

"But we already have a tree house," said Susan, looking a her brother disapprovingly. "And *you don't.*"

Becky looked sharply at Susan. *Susan was just being mean because he was her brother.* "Why do you want to build with us?"

"Because..." started Tim, "You seem to know what you are doing and you are doing a great job." Tom elbowed him in the ribs and gave him a warning look. *Praising the girls?*

Tom added "And because we can't build on our side any more – yours is the only one left."

"And there are no other trees to build in," added Tim.

No More Nails!

Amanda leaned back and crossed her arms. She could choose to be mean like Susan had been, but she had another idea. "It depends."

James looked at her hopefully. "Depends on what?"

Amanda leaned forward, looking serious. "If you want to work with us on the tree house, *you have to pay the price*. All of us girls did." She leaned back and gave them a thin smile.

Tim and Tom exchanged glances. They didn't like the sound of that.

"And add all of your wood to ours," said Alice.

"...um, what is the price?" asked James, uncertainly.

"You will see. But it doesn't take any money. Do you want to build a tree house with us or not?" asked Amanda.

"We do!" said Tim.

Tom looked at his brother. "Yeah, I guess, we do."

James nodded gratefully. "Yes, please."

Amanda looked around at the girls, who slowly nodded in turn. She turned back towards the boys. "Ok then, let's get started. Summer is not that far away. But first things first. *You* are helping *us*. We will work on this tree house together, the seven of us – but you boys have to follow *my* rules."

The boys looked at each other quickly. *Oh no, not another Ben*...thought Tom. She led them over to the kitchen table and started organizing the papers. The boys slowly followed and the seven children gathered around the table.

It turned out "Amanda's Rules" were nothing like working with Ben. She explained the basic ideas her father had taught her (and the girls had improved upon) - **Think-Plan-Do-Finish Up**, about having an idea and thinking about it, planning what you wanted to do, doing it and checking to make sure you had done what you planned. The other girls added further details on how they had improved on Amanda's father's ideas.

"We are still planning and doing, but doing it in small stages," she explained. "We plan each section of the tree house, draw our ideas and discuss them, measure everything, and then take only the wood and tools we need for that *phase*. Then we can put it together pretty quickly, too."

Tim nodded. He liked the idea of that. He had tried drawing a design with the other boys but they had called him silly. *Guess who is silly now*, he thought.

Tom frowned and James rubbed his head, trying to follow along. "You'll get it, just pay attention and watch how we do it," assured Becky, patting James on the shoulder. "Besides, you probably have some good ideas too. We are stuck on how to make railings for the platforms..."

The next Saturday morning, the seven tree house builders converged on the edge of the park – some carrying boards, some carrying tools, but they all had agreed on the plan for the week and how they were going to build the next section – including a solution for the railings. Now that they had more wood available to use, there were more possibilities in what they could do together.

"Oh darn, I forgot the nails!" said James. "I'll run and go get them now." The girls had just about run out of nails – they only had about twenty left. James had offered to supply them, as a kind of peace offering. He ran off towards his house.

When he arrived at home, James headed straight into the garage to find his father putting tools away that were sitting on the workbench. The cabinet door was wide open. James stopped short. "I decided that I had better get started on my spring projects before it gets too hot," said James' father. He sat down on the stool and looked at James.

"But it turns out I can't start on my project. Do you know why?"

James was staring at the open cabinet – where there was only the one bag of nails left on the middle shelf. He forced himself to look into his father's disapproving stare. "Um, no..."

"I think you do. You know, I thought you kids were building with some pretty nice nails when we had to take sections of your tree house apart. I wondered which parent was nice enough to give you all of those nails to build your tree house."

James shifted uncomfortably.

"Imagine my surprise today, when I started to setup the tools for my weekend project and found out that they were *my* nails!" He looked sternly at James. "Can you explain how you got your nails?"

James swallowed hard. "Um, well, I, um...*borrowed them*?"

James' father smacked his hand down on the workbench. "**Borrowed!** James, I am disappointed. If you had *asked me*, I may have given you a couple of bags of nails towards your project, or bought you some of your own to use. But you took them *without permission*, and now I have a wasted morning because I have to go and buy more nails so I can do my project. Not to mention - they were not cheap nails!"

James was suddenly feeling sick, but he had to ask. "So, um, I guess I can't have any more nails?"

"**No**, you can't. You were dishonest, and there is a price to pay for that. And such a waste too – we had to pull so many bent nails out of that tree house and throw them away," he shook his head. "You and your friends will have to find your nails somewhere else. I have to go to the store now – and I guess I will have to start locking the cabinet. I am very disappointed in you."

James slumped out of the garage and walked back towards the park, empty handed.

"What happened? Where are the nails?" asked Amanda.

James shrugged, and explained what had happened. "You were **stealing**??" exclaimed Becky. She shook her head and then turned her back to James. "The rest of us asked our parents for stuff. We got *permission*," she said over her shoulder.

James just hung his head.

The Ultimate Tree House *Project!*

Amanda pulled out a small roll of papers from her pocket. She studied them for a moment, and then announced "Well, we can get started anyway and make some progress. In the meantime…" she turned to look at James. "*You* need to figure out how we can get some more nails, but *with permission* this time."

They all walked over to the edge of the park and on into the forest. James sniffed.

They unloaded their supplies underneath the girls' tree house, and then Tim, Tom and Alice went over to the boys' pile to find some boards of the right size for the next phase of the project. James stood there thinking, watching the work going on around him, and then looked up into the tree. He was still feeling sick from what he had done. His nose was dripping a little and a small bubble of snot formed when he breathed out. He gave a loud sniff to try to pull it back in. It was sticky, messy stuff. It was…*sticky*!

"I have an idea!" shouted James. "We might not need any more nails."

The other children gathered around him, looking dubious. They were not sure they trusted him just yet. "You know that super glue stuff they advertise on TV, the stuff that will make anything stick to anything?" He looked around at their faces. "Maybe we can make our own superglue!"

No More Nails!

"With what?" asked Alice. Becky did not feel like talking to him at the moment, and just glared at him.

"Well, you know something really sticky might work," he looked at them. They looked back, not comprehending. "Something sticky that we *make ourselves*." They just stared at him blankly.

"Like paper mache, like we do in class?" asked Susan.

James shook his head. 'Something that we have *right here, right now*."

They all looked around. The only thing they could see was the tree, the ground, the pile of wood and each other. "What is it?"

"I think I will have to show you. Please give me two pieces of wood," asked James.

Tim and Tom held out two pieces of wood in front of James. "OK, here goes..." He stuck his finger up his nose as far as it would go, and snorted. When he pulled out his finger it was covered in greenish goo.

"Boogers!" cried Tim. Tom was speechless.

"Oh, that is soooo gross!" exclaimed Amanda.

Alice pretended to vomit. "Yuck!"

Susan just said "You wait until I tell Mom what you just did!"

Becky looked first at the boards, then at James' booger-covered finger, shuddered and turned away.

"C'mon, hold up the boards," James commanded.

Tim held up one board while James wiped most of the booger onto one end. "Ok, now put the other board on it and press hard." The twins did.

"How long does it take?" asked Tim.

"I don't know, this is the first time I tried it," said James. On one of Dad's wood glue bottles it says it takes ten to fifteen minutes to set."

Tim and Tom carefully set the boards on the ground, gross bits still touching. They didn't want to hold it for that long - especially covered in booger.

"Or, maybe it is like contact cement," suggested James, "Where you have to wet both parts and let them partly dry. Please grab two more boards." Tim and Tom went to get two more boards. James stuck his finger up his other nostril and blew. Bits of snot flew out past his finger and landed on his shoe.

"I don't think letting the boys help us was such a great idea," shuddered Alice. "They are sooooo gross!"

No More Nails!

Meanwhile, James had carefully wiped half of the booger on one piece of board and spread it around, and then repeated it on the other board. "Ok, now we will let it dry for a few minutes."

They stood looking at the two pairs of booger-covered boards lying on the ground. James counted to a hundred. "Ok, let's put the ends together and stand on it. Sometimes Dad even gives it a whack with a hammer." Tim lifted one board and set it on the other, and then Tom stood on the end. The girls stood well back from this performance.

"It's a dumb idea," muttered Becky.

Tom looked at the boards and told Tim he could step off it. "Ok let's see if it worked." He lifted one of the first set of boards and it separated easily, though there were strings of booger stretching from one piece to the other. "Let's try the next boards," said James. He lifted one of the other boards and it pulled away easily, but this time there was no thread of boogers. "Nuts!" he said. "I was sure it would work."

Amanda was unimpressed. "You just ruined *four* boards. No way those ones are going up into *our* tree house. Take them over to the fallen tree and keep them away from the clean wood pile." James picked up two of the boards and carried them over to the fallen tree and dropped them. He came back for the next pair.

Nobody wanted to help him carry the booger-soaked boards.

"That was really, *really* gross," stated Amanda. "OK then, back to work. James will have to come up with another idea – that *does not* involve spit, boogers or any other bodily fluids!"

No More Nails!

16. Lemonade, Sir?

James pitched in and helped the others get the new boards up into the tree. They only had enough nails to secure five boards, so they finished up around 10am. They stacked the extra boards in the middle of the main platform, placing them close together so that no one would trip on them. The children took turns climbing down the rope ladder. The boys went a little slower, admiring the working rope ladder.

When they were all on the ground, Amanda turned to look at the group – and at James. "OK then, do you have any other ideas?" she looked at him sternly. "…And remember I told you, no gross ones!"

James shook his head. Everything he could think of was probably weird, or gross – to girls, anyway.

Lemonade, Sir?

Becky spoke up. "We could raise some money so we can buy some more nails."

"Great idea – anyone have a suggestion on how we can make some money quickly?" asked Amanda.

"We can have a garage sale!" said Tom.

"Let's bake cookies!" said James.

Susan snorted. "More like eat the cookies, you mean."

James stuck out his tongue at his sister.

Tim was thinking, scratching his toe in the dirt. "How about we sell lemonade? It's a hot day, and everyone likes lemonade when it's hot. Also, it doesn't take long to make and we can start selling it right away!"

"Great idea!" Amanda nodded her head. "We have some lawn chairs and a small table and umbrella. Each of you go home and see if your parents will let you bring stuff for lemonade – powder, water bottles, jugs, ice, spoon, a cooler, plastic cups and stuff. Everybody meet at my house and we'll get started. But…" she frowned at James, "make sure you get *permission*!"

Thirty minutes later, they had all assembled outside of Amanda's house. Tim had also brought some cardboard and a permanent marker to make a sign. "Good thinking, Tim!" nodded Amanda approvingly.

The others were getting started on mixing up the lemonade. "How much should we charge?" asked Tim.

"How much is a bag of nails?" asked Alice.

"I dunno, maybe ten dollars?" said James.

"OK then, let's say one dollar per cup, and then we only need to sell ten cups to make enough for one bag. If we sell more then we can save it towards the next bag, because we may need more than one bag of nails," said Alice.

Tim wrote on the sign:

Ice Cold Lemonade: $1

He walked around to the front of the table and leaned it against the leg of the table, so it could

Lemonade, Sir?

be easily seen from the road and the playground. A couple dozen kids were playing there.

After a few minutes, two boys from the playground came wandering over. "How much is the lemonade?" asked one of the boys.

Becky pointed to the sign. "One dollar per cup."

The first boy shook his head. "That's too much. I don't have that much money at home."

Becky replied firmly, "One dollar per cup."

The two boys walked back to the playground, empty-handed.

A little while later three little girls came over, read the sign and left. "Too much!" they said.

It was getting hotter and the lemonade was starting to warm up. They needed to start selling it soon. Nobody would want to buy *warm* lemonade.

"Change the price, quick!" said Amanda. "Make it fifty cents."

Tim went around the table and wrote on the sign, just as another two kids from the park came walking over. The sign now read:

Ice Cold Lemonade: $1~~ 50cents

They read the sign and dug into their pockets. They each had 50 cents and handed the money over to Becky, who was running the cash box (an empty piggy bank from her bedroom).

Pretty soon, there was a swarm of children coming to buy lemonade. Many of them went home to get money and came running back. Becky's piggy bank was starting to get heavy, as the others quickly mixed up jug after jug of lemonade and poured it out into the cups for the thirsty crowd.

Within an hour, the cooler was empty of ice and all their bottles of water were gone. They had about half a jug of lemonade left, which Alice poured out evenly into seven cups so they could all have a taste. Becky stuffed the last coin into the top of the piggy bank.

Once they had emptied their cups, Amanda smiled at everyone. "Well done! Now, let's see how much money we made."

Becky opened the bottom of the piggy bank and shook the coins out onto the table. All of the children helped stack the coins into even piles so they could be counted more easily. Alice then began counting the piles. When she was finished, she said "We have twelve dollars and fifty cents."

Lemonade, Sir?

Becky had been counting as well and finished just after Alice. "Yep, twelve-fifty."

"Hopefully that is enough for a good sized bag of nails," said Amanda. "Let's go find out!" She went back inside to ask her mother if they could walk down to the hardware store together.

"As long as you stay together – but have your friends asked their parents?" replied her mother.

Amanda came back outside. "Quick run home and ask if we can walk to the hardware store together to buy some nails. We still have a chance to finish what we started today if we hurry."

The children scattered off to their houses, taking the things they had brought for the lemonade stand. Amanda folded up the umbrella and took it inside, then returned for the little table and the lawn chair. By the time she had finished, Alice, Tim and Tom were waiting outside. A couple of minutes later, the rest of them showed up. Susan had a smile on her face. "Dad paid us our allowance," she said. "I told him we were selling lemonade to buy nails. He said that was good, but we might need some help. So here it is." Susan gave Becky the money in her hand. "He gave me two dollars."

James pulled his hand out of his pocket. "Dad only gave me one dollar this week," he said and passed the money to Becky.

"You were lucky to get *anything* this week," frowned Susan.

As it turned out, Tim and Tom had been given some allowance too. When they added up their lemonade stand earnings and the allowance money, they had eighteen dollars and fifty cents between them.

"Let's go buy some nails!" said Becky.

The seven tree house builders then walked on down the street to the hardware store.

They returned to the tree about an hour later, with two bags of nails and a little change left over.

"I didn't know they had sales on nails," said Tim. "I guess we lucked out today!"

The children were buzzing with excitement as Susan lowered the rope ladder and they climbed the ladder to continue working on the tree house together.

Lemonade, Sir?

17. Finishing Touches

Over the next few weeks, the tree house builders fell into a regular routine. They would finish their homework quickly during the week and then go over to Amanda's and spend as much time as they could before dinner. They worked on the planning details for what they would build the coming weekend. They had a few disagreements, but the girls and boys all agreed that the plans they ended up with were good, and some were much better than the ones the girls had come up with on their own. "Great teamwork!" Amanda frequently remarked.

With the extra wood, plenty of nails and now seven builders, they could get a lot more done at once. The girls even agreed to some of the ideas the boys had – a comic room sounded reasonable, and a spyglass for a lookout was actually pretty cool, but they were not so sure about a bowling alley up in the tree. They agreed to test the idea a bit later, with some tennis balls and small sticks on an existing platform.

They had also unanimously agreed with Tim's suggestion that they would take a break from building every Saturday for an hour or so to sell lemonade. "The extra money will come in handy, and besides we will get thirsty and we like lemonade too."

Amanda had added another section to one of the pieces of paper to keep track of the lemonade money they earned and the money they spent on nails and a few other things. *Income* and *Expenses*, her father had called it.

By the end of the third week of working together, the tree house was starting to look *fantastic*. There were now eight separate platforms of different sizes and at four different heights. A couple of the platforms were only big enough to hold one or two people. There were also railings around most of the platforms – some of them were made of wood, and others were made of rope tied to posts at the corners. They had built a few more rope ladders inside the tree to get around the different platforms more easily, but these ones were tied at both the top and the bottom.

They tested the bowling alley idea and did some measurements. It would be no problem to add sides to a platform to keep the ball from falling to the ground, but length was an issue. They could not make a long enough platform because they ran into two problems – they only had a few fence rails left, and they would need several branches all lined up together, and *flat* – and they couldn't find any. Tim looked a bit sad when they had worked that part out, but Alice saved the day. "We can still have a bowling alley, and it can be as long as we want!" she said.

Tim and Tom turned to look at her, confused. "But…we just measured and everything and we can't make a proper bowling alley in the tree. It's *impossible*," said Tom.

"Well, *in the tree*, yes. But who said it actually needs to be in the tree? The ground under the tree is nice and flat, and we have all those fence posts we haven't used yet. We could use those to make the edges of the bowling alley," smiled Alice.

"But those boards are *heavy*," complained Tim. "How are we supposed to lift them? We tried lifting them before."

Alice was persistent. "How many of you tried to lift a fence post?"

"Um, well just two of us, I guess," replied Tim.

"…and there are how many of us now?" asked Alice.

Finishing Touches

Tim was thoughtful. "Seven. But do you think we can lift them?"

"Only one way to find out," interrupted Susan. "Let's go try it now!"

Together, they walked out into the back yard, where there were only a handful of boards left, other than the stack of fence posts. One way or another, their project was going to have to end soon. They were running out of materials.

"OK, how do we do it?" asked Tom.

"Boys on one side, girls on the other," directed Susan. The boys moved to the side opposite the girls. "Ok, bend down and grab the top post with both hands, lift on the count of three. Ready?"

The other children all nodded. "OK, 1…2…3…lift!"

Together, they lifted the fence post easily. Tim laughed out loud. "This is *light*!" He looked at the fence post doubtfully. "Are you sure this is the same fence post?"

Susan nodded. "That's what you get from *teamwork*. My mother always says that many hands make light work. I guess this is what she is talking about."

They carefully lowered the fence post and put it back on the pile. All of the children were smiling.

The Ultimate Tree House *Project!*

On Saturday morning, they brought the tools and boards over to the tree to assemble the 9th and final platform. There were only a few boards left; they were still deciding what to do with them, but there were not enough boards for another platform. *Some extra railings, maybe, or just spare boards*, thought James.

A couple of hours later, they had finished the final platform. They had secured the railings and installed another rope ladder leading up to it. This was the "penthouse" – the fifth level of the tree house. "OK team, time for lemonade, lunch – and then we set up the bowling alley!" They had all agreed to leave that for the last, as a kind of "finishing touch".

The team of tree house builders walked through the park, smiling and chatting. The children in the playground looked up at them and waved. It was now a routine – some of the playground children waved coins in the air, while others who had forgotten quickly ran home to get their 50 cents.

By the time the seven friends had the lemonade stand setup and the first jug mixing, there was already a large line-up of smiling, thirsty children, coins in hand.

Finishing Touches

After lunch, the children assembled in the back yard by the stack of fence posts. They lined up like they had done before, boys on one side, girls on the other. Ben was watching from his bedroom window. His cast had been taken off last Friday, but he still had to take it easy. He was not allowed to go to the tree house, because he needed some time to strengthen the muscles in his left leg. Alice waved up at him. Ben closed the curtain. Alice just shook her head.

Susan was ready to go. "OK everyone? Like we did before. On three. 1…2…3…lift!"

The seven children lifted the fence post and carried it out through the gate, across the street and through the park. They walked past the fallen tree and over to the tree house. They lowered the fence post carefully so nobody got pinched fingers, and then they stood up. "Not sore at all!" exclaimed Tim.

"It was pretty easy, wasn't it?" said Amanda. "OK, let's go get the rest of the fence posts."

They made eight more easy trips to bring the rest of the fence posts to the tree. They had decided to bring them all and fit them together when they got to the tree. If any boards were left over, they decided they would be used as seating for those watching the game. In the end, they used eight fence posts to form the ends and sides of the bowling alley, with the last one put back a few paces for seating.

When the seating had been put in place, Tim went over to his backpack and pulled out three tennis balls and ten small sticks for bowling pins. He rolled the tennis balls over to one end, and walked to the far end to setup the "bowling pins". When he was finished, he stood up, brushed his hands together and announced "Who wants to be the first to try out the bowling alley with me?"

Six hands shot into the air.

Finishing Touches

172

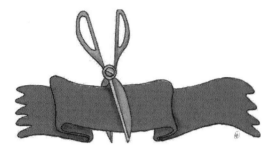

18. Grand Opening

They held the "Grand Opening" two weeks after Ben had his cast taken off. They had to do a lot to get ready, as it turned out. Becky collected the comics together from everyone and put them in a plastic clip container she had got from her mother – *with permission*, for them to keep in the tree so the comics would stay dry. Amanda led Tim, Tom and Alice in checking over the tree house to make sure that no nails were sticking up, all the rope ladders were secure and the railings were still holding. The branches moved a bit with the wind, so it looked like this was something they would have to do every week.

Susan, James and Becky worked at ground level, tidying up bits of wood and putting them into neat piles near the trunk of the tree. They even tried to clean up the "other side" of the tree, where the fallen tree still lay through the branches of the big tree.

Most of the boards had been pulled down and the unbroken ones re-used, but there were still some bits of broken board lying around the fallen tree. They picked these up and added them to the pile. James also had to pick up the four "booger boards" and add them to the throwaway pile. Nobody believed him when he said they were clean now. So, onto the pile they went. *Ick!*

They no longer called it "the boys' side of the tree", because that just didn't seem right anymore – the tree house was now *theirs*, the boys and girls equally. They also had enough platforms that everyone had enough room for a "boys' side" and "girls' side" if they wanted, but they spent a lot of time together in the comic room, either borrowing or returning them to the plastic container. So mostly, it was just *The Tree House*.

They each took some time to make invitations to the Grand Opening. Their parents and brothers and sisters were all invited.

When the day came for the Grand Opening, the tree house team led their parents to the big tree, along with Ben. He was doing pretty good, but his mother walked beside him just in case he needed a hand.

The Ultimate Tree House *Project!*

They all gathered by the bowling alley while Susan lowered the rope ladder. The parents (and Ben) looked around at the bowling alley and up into the tree, where they could make out three or four of the platforms.

When Susan had the rope ladder ready, she pulled a length of ribbon from her pocket and tied it to the rope on either side. She motioned Amanda over and handed her a small pair of safety scissors. Tim, Tom, James, Alice, Becky and Susan moved off to the side behind Amanda, facing their parents. Ben stood uncertainly beside his mother. Amanda waved him over. "C'mon!" she whispered. Ben joined his sister and friends and turned to face their parents.

"The Tree House Team welcome you to the Grand Opening of..." Amanda paused for dramatic effect. "...the *Ultimate Tree House!*"

She lifted the scissors and carefully cut the small ribbon. "The Tree House is now open for visitors!"

Their parents clapped loudly while all the children smiled.

"Who wants to go first?" asked Amanda.

All of the adults held up their hands.

Ben sighed and looked down at the ground. "Ben first!" said Amanda. "*Ben first! Ben first!*" chorused the other children. Ben looked up at his sister, his cheeks turning red at the attention. She just smiled and said "Go on, get up there and look. We even made a platform for you."

Ben looked at her as if to say, *Did you really do that?* But instead of saying anything he grabbed the rope ladder and started climbing up. As soon as he stepped onto the platform, Amanda started to climb up after him. She was only half-way up when they all heard Ben exclaim "**Oh wow – this is sooo cool!"**

After they had shown Ben around the tree house, they let the parents up, one at a time. Each remarked on some feature of the tree house. The spyglass was popular, and there were a number of compliments on the rope ladders and clever railings. "Safety first!" said Susan.

When it was her father's turn, Amanda showed him around the tree house herself. He took his time, inspecting the construction of the tree house while Amanda chatted on about how they had all designed this platform and that rope ladder, and other details. Her father nodded, and continued his inspection. When they were back on the main platform by the rope ladder, he turned to Amanda and patted her on the shoulder. "Amazing. What you kids have built is truly amazing. Well done."

Amanda beamed. "It was *teamwork*, Dad, and *planning*. And also thanks to our *Secret Weapon*," she said as she gave him a big hug.

Grand Opening

19. Tickets, Please

The next Saturday the children were relaxing in the tree house, now that all of the hard work was finished. Most of them were on one platform or another, reading comics. Tim was down in the comic room, putting the one he had just read back in the box, when he heard a noise. No, it wasn't *a noise* – it was *several* noises. And not just a noise, it was voices!

He hurried down to the spyglass and looked through it. What he saw made him gasp. Children were coming into the woods and walking towards their tree house. Not one or two children, but *a lot* of children, maybe fifteen or twenty. "Hey everyone!" he said in a loud whisper. "We have company!"

"What's up?" asked James as he came up beside Tim.

"Look!" hissed Tim.

Tickets, Please

James looked through the spyglass. He didn't actually need to look through the spyglass as he could already see the mass of children coming towards them with his own eyes, *but hey – if you have a spyglass, why not use it? It's pretty cool…*

He was interrupted by Tim. "What do we do?"

Susan appeared beside them. "I'll tell you what we need to do – *prepare to repel boarders!*"

Amanda came down onto the platform. They figured it could safely hold five people, but they didn't want to push it. "I'll go down and see what they want."

She climbed down the rope ladder to greet the visitors. It looked like every child from the playground was there. "What do you want?" she asked.

"Lemonade!" they chorused, and waved their coins in the air.

"I'm sorry, but we are not doing lemonade any more. We are done now."

"Done what?" asked Sam, who had just turned five years old.

"Their tree house, dummy," said his seven year old brother Robby.

"Can I see?" asked Sam.

"No, it's our tree house. And you are too little," replied Amanda.

Sam's lower lip began to quiver. "But *I wanna see it*!"

"How about if we pay for a tour?" asked Robby.

Alice had climbed down the rope ladder and was standing beside Amanda. "Interesting idea," she said. She whispered in Amanda's ear. Amanda's eyes opened wide and she smiled.

"How about fifty cents for a guided tour?" suggested Amanda.

"Yes! Yes!" called the children, waving their coins in the air. Amanda sighed. "Alright, but two at a time, and if you are little that means with your older brother or sister. Stick with us and hold on - It is a long way up and we don't want anyone to fall."

Sam smiled and handed fifty cents to Amanda, then held Robby's hand. "Ready!" Robby put his fifty cents in Amanda's hand and smiled.

"This way!" said Alice as she steadied the rope ladder and helped Sam and Robby onto the ladder, with Robby close behind Sam, helping him up.

Tickets, Please

When Sam and Robby reached the main platform, the children below heard "Oh wow, *oh wow*!"

The playground children all raised their hands excitedly, coins glinting in their hands. "Me next! Me next!"

Amanda looked up at the spyglass platform. "**Tim**!" she called out, "We are going to need a new sign!"

20. Pizza!

With the money they had left over from the lemonade sales, plus the money from the tree house tours, the eight friends calculated that they would have enough to buy four pizzas and a few comics. They decided to get together at Amanda's house the next Saturday and have a pizza party. They were also going to make plans for the summer holidays, which were only a couple of weeks away.

The kids were sitting around the kitchen table, mouths full of pizza when Amanda's father came into the kitchen. "Hello, children," he said.

"Hi Mr. Jones," they said together.

"How is the tree house?" he asked.

"Great!" replied James.

Pizza!

"Cool!" said Tim and Tom together.

"Super!" said Becky.

Amanda's father smiled. "I was wondering if I could talk to you kids for a few minutes?" he raised his eyebrows. Amanda nodded, her mouth still full of pizza.

"OK, well I won't take very long. When our work projects finish, we usually talk about the project while we share a good meal." He looked at the nearly-empty pizza boxes on the table. "We spend a little time talking about what we thought went well, and what didn't. We call this a *lessons learned* session. We use this to help make our next projects even better."

He looked around the table. The children were all looking at him, listening. "Can you think of some things that worked really well, and some that didn't?"

"The Girls' rope ladder was cool," said James.

"Boards can break," grimaced Ben.

"We got a lot done when we worked together," offered Susan.

"The boys had some really good ideas," said Becky.

"So did the girls," added Tim.

"If you don't plan sometimes you have to start again," muttered Tom, thinking about the *safety inspection*.

"Things were a lot easier when we planned stuff first," suggested Amanda.

"It was a lot of fun with all of us working together instead of separately," finished Alice.

Amanda's father smiled. "Well done. Some very good lessons, and I am very impressed with your tree house. After you finish eating, you might want to write those lessons down so you don't forget them later."

He turned and walked to the doorway that led into the living room, where the TV could just be heard behind him.

"I just have one more question for you," he said, as he turned back and looked around at each of the children at the table. "Now that you have finished a successful project, and have what looks like a great team, what is going to be your *next project*?"

The children looked at each other, surprised.

...Their NEXT project?

Did you like this book? Please leave a comment or review on Amazon:

Pizza!

http://www.amazon.com/Ultimate-Tree-House-Project/dp/1482558130

Check out the website for fun activities and projects!

www.theultimatetreehouseproject.com

Coming Soon! Follow the **Project Kids** in their next big adventure, ***The Scariest Haunted House Project Ever***! (Project Kids Adventure #2)

Next: The Scariest Haunted House Project Ever!

The Project Kids are back at school after a long summer of enjoying their Ultimate Tree House. Amanda, Becky and Susan are now in A.J Wilkins Middle School, which is just next door to their old Primary school. This year, the principals of both schools have decided to hold a joint Halloween contest – to see which groups of children from both schools can make the best Halloween display. The eight Project Kids – Becky, Alice, Amanda, Susan, Ben, James, Tim & Tom embark on their *bravest* adventure yet – to come up with the *Scariest Haunted House* – ever. The kids get started on the project and learn that it is not just Haunted Houses that can be scary!

187

Parent/Teacher Note:

With one successful project behind them, the children learn and apply more "project stuff" as they continue to grow on their project adventures. This next book introduces the concept of budgets and managing change and requirements, while reinforcing the skills and lessons they learned on the Ultimate Tree House Project.

www.thescariesthauntedhouseproject.com

The Project Kids Team

James Cartwright

Age: 10

Height: 56 inches (142cm)

Eyes: Brown

Hair: Dark Blonde

Likes: Comic books, Computer games, Building stuff

Dislikes: Dogs that bite, New shoes

Skills: Running, Climbing, Swimming, Building

More info: www.projectkidsadventures.com/James

Ben Jones

Age: 10

Height: 57 inches (145cm)

Eyes: Brown

Hair: Dark Brown

Likes: Being in charge

Dislikes: Big sisters, Planning stuff

Skills: Telling people to do stuff, Having great ideas

More info:

www.projectkidsadventures.com/Ben

Tim O'Reilly

Age: 10

Height: 55 inches (140cm)

Eyes: Green

Hair: Red (Curly)

Likes: Drawing

Dislikes: Bullies

Skills: Working together Fundraising, Perseverance

More info:

www.projeckidsadventures.com/Tim

Tom O'Reilly

Age: 10

Height: 55 inches (140cm)

Eyes: Green

Hair: Red (Curly)

Likes: Computer games

Dislikes: Splinters

Skills: Working together, Lifting people, Perseverance

More info:

www.projectkidsadventures.com/Tom

Amanda Jones

Age: 11

Height: 59 inches (150 cm)

Eyes: Green

Hair: Dark Brown

Likes: Working together with her friends, Girl Guides

Dislikes: Bossy people, Brothers who keep secrets

Skills: Planning, Setting goals, Leadership, Tying knots

More info:

www.projectkidsadventures.com/Amanda

Susan Cartwright

Age: 11

Height: 58 inches (147 cm)

Eyes: Blue

Hair: Blonde

Likes: Nature, hiking

Dislikes: Little brothers, Bees

Skills: Lifting really heavy stuff, Using a compass

More info:

www.projectkidsadventures.com/Susan

Becky Petrov

Age: 11

Height: 56 inches (142cm)

Eyes: Brown

Hair: Brown

Likes: James (kinda), Making rope ladders

Dislikes: People who tell fibs, People being sad or scared

Skills: Climbing, Tying knots, Measuring

More info:

www.projectkidsadventures.com/Becky

Alice Wong

Age: 10

Height: 55 inches (140cm)

Eyes: Brown

Hair: Black

Likes: Cooperating with others, Drawing, Playing with her friends

Dislikes: Messes, Spiders

Skills: Drawing and sketching, Organizing things

More info: www.projectkidsadventures.com/Alice

Glossary

CLOSEOUT Phase (Finish Up) – This is the end of the project, where we make sure that everything we wanted to do for the project is complete.

CONTROL Phase (Lead, Check & Correct) – This is checking that we are still working to the plan, and making corrections if we start to wander off or get distracted by other things. It also includes working with people to make sure they have what they need to get their tasks done, and that people are getting along. The Project Manager spends a fair bit of time doing this.

DEPENDENCY – When one activity (or task) cannot start until another one is finished, there is a dependency on the first task. In the diagram (A->B), B cannot start before A finished because B is dependent on A.

EXECUTION Phase (Do) – This is when the "real" work of the project begins, and most of the building/doing activity happens.

EXPENSE – Money you spend. The children spent money on nails, pizza and a few other things.

INCOME – Money you earn. The money COMEs IN to you. The children earned income by selling lemonade.

INITIATION Phase (Idea/Think) – In the Initiation phase of the project, we have an idea about what we want to accomplish – what we want to do. ("Let's build a tree house!")

LESSONS LEARNED SESSION – At the end of the project (and in the middle of long projects), the team meets to talk about what parts went well, which did not go so well and discuss ideas on how they might do things better next time.

PLANNING Phase (Plan) – During the planning phase of the project, we figure out what needs to be done - in detail - and decide how we are going to do it. ("What should the tree house look like and how are we going to build it?")

PROJECT – A project is a temporary activity with a defined goal, a beginning and an end.

PROJECT MANAGEMENT – Project Management is the application of knowledge, skills, tools and techniques to project activities to meet the project requirements.

REQUIREMENTS – What do we want to have as the results of our project? How many levels? How many rope ladders? What should they look like? …and so on.

RESOURCES – Materials, tools, people or money needed to complete the project. The Project Kids team has eight people, they used wood for the tree house, they used tools, they had to make money to buy nails – these are all examples of resources.

SEQUENCE – The order in which something occurs compared to another thing. For example, A comes before B, B comes before C in the alphabet – that is a sequence. (A->B->C)

SKILL – Knowing how to do an activity, like climb a tree, tie knots, and so on.

TARGET DEADLINE – This is when you want a task or even the entire project to be complete. The kids wanted to have the tree house completed by the end of school so that they could enjoy it all summer.

TASK – An assignment or activity to get a specific part of the project completed – like drilling holes in wood, or installing a rope ladder.

VARIABLES – These are "unknown" things we may need to plan for – like the length of a rope ladder, or how many levels the tree will support. However we don't know at the beginning what they are exactly, and they can change over time.

VISION – The "big picture idea" of what you are trying to do, whether it is building a tree house, painting a picture or something else.

Notes for Parents and Teachers

This book introduces children to a number of basic project management concepts (or simply *project concepts*, if you prefer).

Resources and Downloads

www.projectkidsadventures.com/resources

School Curriculum Applicability

The concepts covered in this book include independent learning and aspects of technology, specifically:

- Characteristics of technology and technological outcomes.

- Technological modelling, products and systems.

- Planning, identifying resources, skills and stages required to complete an outcome.

The relevant school curriculum standards include, at a minimum:

New Zealand

The New Zealand Curriculum (2007),
Technology

- Nature of Technology [Level 1,2]

- Technical Knowledge [Level 1,2]

- Technological Practice [Level 1,2]

Australia

Australian Curriculum [ACARA], **Science**

Year 5

- ACSHE083 – Scientific understandings, discoveries and inventions are used to solve problems

- ACSIS088 – Uses equipment and materials safely, identifying potential risks

- ACSIS093 – Communicates ideas, explanations and processes in a variety of ways

Year 6

The Ultimate Tree House *Project!*

- ACSIS101 - Communicates ideas, explanations and processes in a variety of ways

- ACSIS105 - Uses equipment and materials safely, identifying potential risks

United States

National Standards, **Technology**

- NT.K-12.1 Basic operations and concepts

- NT.K-12.6 Technology problem-solving and decision-making tools

United Kingdom

Primary Curriculum

Design and Technology Key Stage 1

1. Developing, planning and communicating ideas (a,b,c,d,e)

2. Working with tools, equipment, materials and components to make quality products (a,c,d,e)

3. Evaluating processes and products (a,b)

5. Breadth of study (a,b,c)

Design and Technology Key Stage 2

Notes for Parents and Teachers

1. Developing, planning and communicating ideas (a,b,c)

2. Working with tools, equipment, materials and components to make quality products (a,b,d,e)

3. Evaluating processes and products (a,b,c)

4. Knowledge and understanding of materials and components (a,b,c)

5. Breadth of study (a,b,c)

Project Management Concepts

Amanda's father leads her through the basic project stages that are common to every successful project, regardless of your preferred terminology or system.

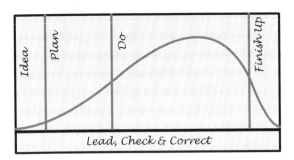

- **Initiation** (Idea / Think)

    - Spring Break is Over! [Boys]

    - The Tree! [Boys]

The Ultimate Tree House *Project!*

- o   The Sky's the Limit! [Boys]

- o   This Means War! [Girls]

- **Planning** (Plan)

- o   Idea, Plan, What? [Girls]

- o   The Plan [Girls]

- o   The Tree Hunt [Girls]

- o   Do We Have Enough Wood? [Girls]

- o   No More Nails! [Both]

- o   Finishing Touches [Both]

- **Execution** (Do)

- o   Ready, Set, Build! [Boys]

- o   Disaster! [Boys]

- o   Do We Have Enough Wood? [Girls]

- o   Girls in the House [Both]

- o   Finishing Touches [Both]

- **Closeout** (Finish Up)

- o   Grand Opening [Both]

- o   Pizza! [Both]

Notes for Parents and Teachers

- **Project Control** (Lead, Check & Correct)

    - The Accident [Boys]

    - Safety Inspection [Both]

    - The Storm [Both]

    - No More Nails [Both]

Note that the boys started out (as we often do), jumping straight in to doing things without any planning or preparation; there are lessons learned around the results of skipping project stages and "just getting on with it"- as shown in Chapter 11, *The Accident*, and Chapter 12 – *Safety Inspection*.

A number of other project concepts are also introduced, either directly or indirectly in the story, including:

- **Requirements** (*Idea, Plan, What? / The Plan / The Tree Hunt*)

- **Estimating / Measurement** (*Do We Have Enough Wood?*)

- **Cost / Budget** (*No More Nails, Lemonade, Sir?, Tickets, Please*)

- **Resource Management** (*No More Nails / Do We Have Enough Wood?*)

- **Teamwork / Human Resource Management** (*Girls in the House / No*

206

The Ultimate Tree House *Project!*

More Nails / Lemonade, Sir? / Finishing Touches / Grand Opening / Pizza!)

- **Change Management** (*The Storm / No More Nails / Lemonade Sir?*)

- **Risk Management** (*The Accident / Safety Inspection*)

The Girls' Project Method

There are a number of project methodologies out there, but when teaching children (or even adults, really), simpler is generally better for starting out. While the project stages apply as a general structure, how projects are structured can differ greatly depending on the circumstances. For example, one project may have a single Think-Plan-Do sequence with all of the planning up front, then all of the doing over a period of time.

Other projects, such as building a tree house, lend themselves to having several smaller phases, each with Think-Plan-Do sequences. When there is a lot of uncertainty, it makes sense to have an overall vision and high level requirements, then plan and do a bit at a time, assess how each step went, and then factor the lessons into the next stage of work.

When the girls built the tree house, they could only measure one level of branches at a time (that was all they could reach!), so they could not do detailed planning for the whole tree house at once. They progressed one level at a time, and also learned how to do each segment better and faster, based on the lessons learned from building the previous levels.

Note: This has many similarities to the **Agile** method of managing projects, where a period of up-front planning is followed by a burst of activity to complete the task, and then they move on to the next piece of planning and work.

About the Author

Gary M. Nelson, PMP (Gazza) is a Project Manager and father of three boys. Gary has worked on projects in New Zealand, Taiwan, Hong Kong, the US and Canada since 1989. He is also the author of Gazza's Guide to Practical Project Management, which uses experience-based stories for grown-up children (i.e. adults) to share project lessons.

Gary loves to tell stories, and is still searching for the perfect tree.

About the Illustrator

My name is Mathew Frauenstein. Amongst other things I enjoy drawing and gaming, so these activities tend to take up most of my free time. However, when I am not doing either of those I will be sleeping, eating or sitting through another day of that horrid activity known as school. At the time of writing this stanza I am living in New Zealand, a very green country known for its friendly natives and its endangered national bird the Kiwi (sadly it cannot fly). However I have not always lived in New Zealand, but rather I was born in South Africa, where the first four years of my life were spent doing what babies normally do: eat, cry, sleep and fill their diapers with gifts for their parents.

Other Books

Project Management (Adult/Bigger Kids)

Gazza's Guide to Practical Project Management, Paperback & eBook

Project Kids Adventures Series

#1 – The Ultimate Tree House Project

Coming Soon:

#2 – The *Scariest* Haunted House Project – *Ever*!

Social Stuff

Book Website:
www.theultimatetreehouseproject.com

Series Website:
www.projectkidsadventures.com

Facebook: TheUltimateTreeHouseProject

Twitter: @ProjectKidsAdv

Email: projectkids@gazzasguides.com

Printed in Great Britain
by Amazon